My Dearest Charlotte

MEAGHAN RAUSCHER

My Dearest Charlotte

Text copyright © 2021 Meaghan Rauscher

Cover design by Cynthia Stuckey | www.happygostuckey.com

First printed in the United States of America in June 2021 by Amazon
ISBN-13: 9780578940021

First Amazon paperback printing, May 2021 ©Meaghan Rauscher

Courtney.
You spent eighteen months in this world without me. I'm blessed to have always had you in my life. Thank you for always pulling me up when I need it most. The term, "older sister" is far too shallow a label for what you are to me. This one is for you.

BOOKS BY MEAGHAN RAUSCHER

DROPLETS TRILOGY

DROPLETS

RIPPLES

TORRENTS

ROAR OF THE REALM SERIES

ROAR OF THE REALM

CHAPTER 1

Not every woman can be Elizabeth Bennet. Someone has to be Charlotte Lucas.

It was a thought I'd had for years, and one that was more apparent than ever as my twenty-seventh year began and my left ring finger was still naked. Charlotte was my kindred spirit, my dear friend. She was my constant companion when I thought of the looming future of loneliness and lack of adventure. She was the poster child of lost dreams, of settling for the small and practical.

I didn't want to be Charlotte, but it seemed to be my lot in life.

I was staring at the back of a bathroom stall door. The white paint was chipped in places to make it look worn and rustic. A ridiculous notion when it was clear this barn was recently built.

I rolled my eyes for the second time in less than a minute. It was my best friend's wedding, set in our rural hometown of Landing, Alabama. It was home to me, but the kind of town where swiping right wasn't an option. Not when you knew every guy in a 100 miles radius, and not when most were already married.

Sighing, I placed my hands on my hips and waited for the women's voices in the bathroom to fade. Why I was hiding from them, I wasn't sure. Maybe it was the glass of wine clouding my mind.

Deep down I knew it had more to do with the steadying breaths I had been taking to ensure I didn't cry. Somehow, someway I would keep all emotion locked tight.

I knew the signs so well. The sharp pangs would steal across my chest and suck my breath away. I could feel when the pressure began to form at the back of my eyes and the tightness lumped in my throat. They were the warning bells to flee. And I did.

I used to hold out, push through, but now, I fled. What a fearful woman I had become, running at the slightest threat of unwarranted tears.

Come on! I thought, wanting to push these women out the door.

At some point, they would have to grow tired of talking about their children, their husbands, the problems of teething babies, and nursing. Digging my fingers into my hips, I waited, all the while knowing I was a hypocrite. If I were them, I would never stop talking about these things. And even now, I didn't. My life was just different than theirs. How could I blame them?

Finally, the door opened, the DJ's voice echoing through the bathroom for a moment. It faded as the door snapped shut. I cautiously stepped out of the stall, adjusting the waistline of the olive, green dress. With a glance at my thick, brown hair and the braided crown running around my head, I wiped at the darkened circles under my eyes, thankful it was only mascara.

One final breath of courage and I left the safety of the bathroom.

The music thrummed as it had all night, pulsing with excitement. I smiled; it was exactly the sort of celebration Kari had talked about since we were kids. She loved to dance, and sure enough there she was in the middle of it all hopping around to the music. A drink was in one hand and a bundle of her dress in the other. She was shouting and laughing—I grinned watching her.

"Danielle!"

I turned, chewing quickly on the huge bite of cake I had just taken, and waved my free hand. "Hey," I said, smiling around the icing while hoping it wasn't coating my teeth as the familiar sight of Mason walked toward me.

Mason. My stomach plummeted in anticipation and nervousness.

Some people filtered in and out of life with little to no impression. Mason wasn't one of them. He'd left an imprint on my heart, even though he'd never known it.

All through middle school and high school he'd been in my group of friends. It was why he was here tonight, and why I had worried so much about my appearance. He was everything tall, husky and light—his blonde hair brightening a darkened room. I'd often wondered about his blue eyes; they were the color of sapphires and when he smiled his teeth flashed in perfect lines.

"How are you?" he asked, the dimples in his tanned cheeks deepening. He'd always had a smile that could warm me. I'd always wondered if he noticed, while simultaneously cursing myself for still behaving like a child.

"Good. Can't complain." I smiled. "Although, not as good as Kari."

He glanced toward the dance floor where Kari was doing her signature side-hop, dance move—arms all akimbo. Where it had started, we never knew, but she always went for it.

"No one can be that good." Mason laughed.

"Agreed," I said, so many thoughts whirling through my mind. An awkward pause was filled in by the pulsing of the music. I took another bite of cake, my eyes wandering from person to person on the dance floor, while frantically trying to think of something to ask Mason.

"Dani!" A hand waved from the middle of the dance floor.

I knew it was Roland before I even looked. Only Roland called me Dani.

I spotted him. The best man of the wedding, his head above most of the crowd as it usually was, and his long, dark hair sticking to his forehead with sweat. He waved for me to come and join them. I laughed and shook my head, no.

He gave me a mock frown, pausing for a moment as the beat held, his eyes wide, then began jumping again when it dropped. I could see he was laughing as he held my gaze and kept waving. I shook my head again, smiling this time. Beside him was Kari's new husband, Joel. Together they bounced to the beat.

Where Roland was long, Joel was short. Where Roland was all things lean and muscular from working in his shop, Joel was soft and round in the middle. They were opposites of one another, but inseparable since Roland's first day of school during our sophomore year.

Roland tapped on his wrist as though reminding me of the time. I held up a finger telling him to wait. He quirked his head to the side and lifted a fist, grinning, his middle finger beginning to slowly rise. I shook my head again, trying to fight back a grin. Before the finger had even begun to unfurl, he laughed and waved it off while jumping to the music, the colored lights pulsing. He would never make that kind of gesture at me—nor would he curse.

Roland was all things gentle. We had an ongoing joke that someday I would hear him curse—one day I would catch him. He'd only smiled when I said that the first time and after ten years, I still hadn't heard him utter one foul word.

As though sensing my thoughts, Roland grinned, his eyes flicking to Mason. He gave me a speculative look. He knew how I felt about Mason and I felt my cheeks flush with heat. He had guessed my feelings about Mason years ago.

Roland winked and I knew that if he had been within reach, I would have elbowed him. His grin grew and he turned away, his sweaty hair flicking to the rhythm.

"Some things never change," Mason said, nearly shouting over the music.

"No, they don't," I said, swallowing down my nervousness. How much of our exchange had Mason noticed? "So, does it feel good to be back?" I asked, still standing awkwardly with my plate of forgotten cake. How I hoped I didn't have icing on my teeth, or that my mouth hadn't turned to the pale yellow of the icing rose I'd eaten.

"It really does, actually." Mason turned toward me, his beer was sweating, just like my feet were sweating in my too high-heeled shoes. "My mom has been so happy to have me back for a whole week. We've done so much. It's been nice to see all our old places."

My heart fell a little. *A week? He'd been back for a week and hadn't told me?*

"That's good you've had so much time with her."

He shrugged, seeming unconcerned. "Yeah, got back on Monday and had some meetings. I've actually decided to move back to Landing."

"Really?" There was a little jolt in my heart.

"Yeah, I'll be back in a few months. You know the old barbershop on Maurel Street? Well, Doctor Stevens is retiring and offered to sell his practice to me. I'm going to have the barbershop renovated and move the practice there." He waved a hand as though it was the simplest thing in the world, but it wasn't, not to me. "Grams isn't doing as well as she used to, and I wanted to be closer to home."

I blinked. "Wow."

It was common knowledge that Kari's father was retiring. The small town of Landing knew he was ready to travel the world, and Kari getting married sealed the deal. Dr. Stevens was leaving, or Dr. Stevo as he preferred to be called.

I wondered why Kari hadn't told me Mason was moving back.

Probably because she has no idea you still like him.

I wrinkled my nose at the thought. It was true I kept that hope locked away, far from the light of day or anyone's knowledge. Except for Roland—but that was only because he asked me about it once. Of course, that was years ago.

"Well, that's exciting. Congrats, Mason."

"Thanks," he smiled, taking a sip of his beer.

"So, do I have to call you Doctor Jones now?"

A bark of laughter was my answer and I beamed. It'd been a joke since we were kids. Mason had always said he was going to be a dentist someday, which had prompted Joel to call him Dr. Jones. It just so happened we were all fans of Indiana Jones, so Mason was at the mercy of our ridiculousness when his last name was the perfect comedic relief. There'd even been a Halloween where he'd become the greatest of icons and dressed as Indiana Jones.

"No one has called me that in years," Mason shook his head, the blue lights flashing over his blonde hair. "Or at least, not in that way."

"What's home for, if not to remind you how dumb you were as a kid?" I shook my head, pleased to hear Mason's chuckle.

The beat of the music slowly shifted as the DJ's voice echoed over the speakers. The dancers all paused and clapped.

"All right ladies and gentleman, it's that time!"

I froze. *No!* I thought I had missed it.

Stepping back unconsciously, I looked for a place to flee. Tears threatened—I hated how broken I was. I should have stayed in the bathroom.

"Can I get all the single ladies out here on the dance floor?" The DJ's voice echoed in the microphone, pounding in my ears. Cheers rang and laughing young women began to walk toward the dance floor.

I used to be one of those, but that was when it had been fun. Back before I was the oldest woman to step on the dance floor. Back when I had caught the bouquet at my other friends' weddings three different times, and everyone had said, "Oh! You're next!" I had laughed then, I didn't now.

Suddenly I realized I was standing all alone. Mason had moved to join the crowd dotted around the edge of the dance floor. Men hollered and women cheered. The photographer's camera clicked away, capturing moments that would be frozen for years. I backed away; my face flushed by my cowardice.

A warm hand touched my shoulder and I nearly flinched. Roland wrapped his fingers around my arm and led me toward the bar.

"Come on, Dani, I need a drink."

I simply nodded as I blocked out the sounds behind me. The DJ was pumping up the music and the crowd cheered. Kari must be putting on a show. I wondered if she would notice I was missing. Probably not. It was her wedding day, and she was entitled to simply enjoy herself.

"A water, please," Roland said, "And?" he looked down at me. It was only then that I saw the lines of concern across his sweaty brow.

"White wine, please," I said and glanced over my shoulder just in time to hear the countdown and the bouquet arc in the air over the crowd. Women screamed and everyone laughed as some blonde girl held the flowers up like a trophy for all to see.

I grimaced at the ridiculousness of it all and turned back to the bar. Roland handed me the glass of wine, his skin brushing against my fingers. "Thank you."

He smiled, but it didn't reach his eyes as he drained his water. "My good man, another," he said, slamming the glass down on the counter. The bartender found Roland less than amusing. "Don't worry, he'll cut me off before I've had too many." Roland winked.

At that, I rolled my eyes. As long as I had known Roland, he'd never had a drink. I'd asked him about it once, but he'd just shook his head. That was so many years ago.

"You're ridiculous, as always," I said, sipping my wine. Roland beamed as I knew he would.

"Good," he said, "because that means nothing has changed."

His words brought back what I had said to Mason about nothing changing. Glancing toward where I had last seen him, I found him gone. Blinking, I searched longer. The DJ was making all sorts of noise again and it was only then that I realized the garter was being tossed. A pack of men stood at the back of the dancefloor, but one held the prize high. *Mason.*

A song started, and Mason pulled the blonde girl with the bouquet onto the dance floor. I watched, the light moving slowly, lazily, as he pulled the girl close and she smiled, her hand resting along his solid arm. She laughed at something he said and he smiled, those blue eyes bright and watching her—mesmerized.

Somehow, right then, I knew.

A piece of me broke inside.

"I have to go," I said, hardly voicing the words. Placing the wine glass on the bar I fled for what felt like the tenth time that day. There in the muggy heat of an unusually warm, November evening, I stood with my back against the barn wall. Light from the windows spilled to either side of me as I stood in the darkness between.

Perhaps it wasn't obvious to others, but I loved Mason. Or at least I thought I did. But I loved him from afar—I always had. Through high school, through college, all those years he'd been in medical school. So many years, hung up on him. And now…I thought of that blonde girl. I didn't know who she was, but I could see it in his eyes. He'd never looked at me that way.

Placing a hand to my forehead, I tried to catch my breath. Somehow, someway I would make it through tonight. Tears threatened as another slow song began inside the barn. It filtered gently out the open doors and into the starlit night.

I heard his footsteps before I saw him.

He moved through the light of one of the windows, meeting me in the dark, his hand extended. I raised my eyes to Roland's, not sure what he wanted.

He cocked his head to the side, his dark eyes warm and confident. That was one thing I always liked about Roland, he was always so confident, so sure of himself.

"What kind of best man would I be if I didn't ask the maid of honor for a dance?"

Some of the weight that was pressing on me lifted. Without a word, I looked down at my feet and kicked off the heeled shoes that hurt my toes. I'd had enough of it all.

Stepping forward, the grass tickled my skin as I placed my hand in his. The sides of his mouth curved up in a gentle smile as he pulled me close, his large hand pressing gently against my back, the other wrapping around my fingers. There we swayed in the dark, neither of us saying a word. Somehow, I knew Roland felt my pain. He always had.

Of all my friends, he was the one to check on me. We were like that, a sort of pair. Neither of us joined in on all the partying in college. We'd often found each other while our friends danced and threw back shots. We'd spent many hours simply talking and keeping one another company while the rest of the world danced on.

But tonight, it was our turn to dance. Our turn to slowly dim the music and for once tune out the world that so often left us behind.

The loneliness began to seep in and I thought of Charlotte Lucas again. Only the Charlotte Lucas's of the world understood what it was like to be overlooked and cast aside. To feel as though the world had forgotten you existed.

Leaning my head onto Roland's chest, I whispered my thanks. His hand on my back drew me a little closer, and the warmth of him seemed to seep into all the parts of me that had grown cold.

CHAPTER 2

"Mayo," I mumbled in disgust and put the sandwich down on my desk. Once again, my order at Baker's Local Deli was wrong. No matter how many times I told Henry that I didn't like mayonnaise, he tended to forget and add it anyway.

I knew if I took it back, he would apologize profusely. It was a mistake made from habit. His signature sandwich always came with mayo, sometimes he simply forgot to stay his hand when it came to mine.

Pursing my lips, I glanced around my home office and toward the kitchen. I knew there was hardly anything in there I would want to eat. Better to leave the "staring in the fridge game" until dinner.

Glancing at my computer, I debated. I knew where I could go to eat and it wouldn't cost me a dime. As though in confirmation, my email remained clear of new messages, and my checklist was crossed off. Of all things, I was ahead of schedule, if that was even possible.

Grabbing a scarf, from one of the hooks on the brick accent wall of my loft, I threw it around my neck. There were some days when I just knew that business wasn't going to happen promptly, and today was one of those days.

I was a web designer, graphic designer, content creator, and writer all wrapped into one. Self-employed and quite successful.

After a short time spent living with my parents after college, I had been able to launch my business. One client led to another and now I was working for medium-range companies from the comfort of my home. According to my younger brother, I had the life.

Of course, what he didn't see were the late-night hours when I hustled against a deadline.

No, all too often I found that people who heard that I was both self-employed, and worked from home, tended to think I worked little to no hours. Perhaps it was because they spotted me at Café Aroma, our local coffee shop, more days than were good for my bank account. But I didn't mind.

Like most things, unless you experience it, you don't understand it. At least that's what my older sister, Anna, had told me once. Though only two years older than me, her wisdom stretched far beyond that. She was more than a sister, more than a friend, a deep bond ran between us, one that couldn't be broken by circumstance.

More often than not, she was my backbone and the helping hand that pulled me back to my feet when I needed it most.

Thudding heavily down the steps from my downtown loft, I slung my leather backpack over my shoulder, the sandwich from Baker's in hand. I knew one person who would eat all the mayo in the world if he could.

A sharp wind tugged at my jacket and I shivered. As muggy and humid as it had been at Kari's wedding, the weather had plummeted, leaving us with a cold holiday season. For once Christmas morning had been chilly, cold enough that I had been able to hold a cup of coffee in my hands while wearing Christmas pajamas and not sweating. A rare feat, depending on the year in the southern states.

The brick wall of Roland's shop loomed around the corner of downtown Landing. I smiled to myself, as I glanced at the mural coating the brick wall. Sometimes there were girls taking photos together or alone, every now and then holding out coffees or doing popular dances for social media. I was finally at that age where I could roll my eyes at it all.

But did it make me a hypocrite if I still spent time scrolling?

Another gust of wind tugged at my coat and seemed to cut through my jeans as I reached the front of Roland's workshop. The simple logo with a saw and his last name, Harmon, was painted on the window. I had designed that logo—it was one of my first jobs. How was I to know it would be a logo recognized throughout the country?

The bell on the custom Dutch door rang as I stepped into the front of the shop.

"Hey Cole," I said, waving a hand at the high school boy who worked behind the counter. He always had a pencil stuck behind his ear but never used it.

"Hey Danielle, how's it going?"

"Can't complain," I called over my shoulder, flashing him a smile he didn't see. If there was one thing I had learned about Cole, it was that he took his job very seriously. He would man that counter with all he was worth. Other than that, I also knew that Roland liked him, he was a hard worker. And hard work went a long way with Roland.

Pushing open the back door, the smell of fresh wood and sawdust assaulted my nose as I stepped into Roland's workshop. The echo of a worship song blared on a blue tooth speaker, and from somewhere behind a stack of wood, I heard the deep humming that so often accompanied this space.

"Roland?" I asked.

"Over here," he called back, his deep voice booming. He must still have his earplugs in, sometimes he forgot to take them out after working the table saw.

I rounded the stack of wood and spotted him inspecting a table leg, his shoulders hunched as he ran his hand over the wood and toward the tabletop. His concentration was absolute. It was what made him so good at what he did—it was what had made a Harmon piece so valuable. *American-made, and handcrafted with precision.*

He'd laughed the first time I'd pitched that simple line for his website, but he wasn't laughing now. Glancing at his workbench I could see the number of orders waiting for production. More and more people wanted a Harmon chair, table, bench, coffee table, or anything else he could make from wood. The problem, and blessing, was he only had two hands. It was a problem because he could only take so many orders. But, demand increased desire, especially where scarcity was concerned. He was the first client I had worked with that had crashed his site, a fact he never failed to bring up.

Once I'd asked him if he would ever out-source his work, but he'd told me that wasn't an option. He liked overseeing everything he made, and already his success had exceeded his expectations. I'd dropped the matter when he told me that to out-source would be to lose the personal touch.

"Hey," Roland said, his voice still too loud.

I tapped my ear and he nodded before removing the earbuds.

"Hey," he said again, his voice lower, the deep sound I had come to know so well making me feel at ease. His eyes ran over me in one swift glance, focusing on my hand where I held the brown bag. "Henry put mayo on your sandwich again?"

I sighed as though it was the greatest tragedy of our time. "Yes, what do you have?"

"Just my classic PB&J."

"My favorite. Trade?" I asked, scrunching my nose.

"Sure, but we share the chips." He took off his protective eyewear and dug into the sandwich I had brought. I smiled to myself. Ever since he'd moved here with his mom in high school, he'd loved Baker's sandwiches.

"How's your day going?" he asked around a bite of roast beef. I worked away at pulling off the crust from the carefully traded peanut butter and jelly sandwich. No matter how many times I was told otherwise, the crust was the worst part. I liked to get it over with and eat it first.

"Can't complain," I shrugged.

Roland rolled his eyes. "Are you back to that already?"

"What?"

"You told me that you were going to start being honest this year."

"I am," I said, taking another bite. "I have a good life, so I can't complain." The excuse was enough to keep him off track. No one could get me to admit my real resolution—to stop running from the things that scared me. To start living.

"Right," he said, his eyes saying otherwise.

"What's with this here?" I asked, pointing to a pile of tools on one of his work tables.

His brow furrowed and he pushed back a chunk of the dark hair that had a habit of falling forward. "Umm, those are tools."

It was my turn to roll my eyes. "Really? I had no idea." Turning from him, I moved closer to the table. "What I meant was, how come they are in my normal spot?" I flashed him a grin.

"Ahh," he said, wiping at the mayo on his hands. Somehow, he had already consumed half of the nine-inch sandwich. I had told him he needed to eat more. He was anything but small, his broad shoulders filling out the gray t-shirt that was slightly damp with his sweat. "See, I would have kept that spot clear, but I knew you would need something to complain about, so I left those there as a service to you."

I pursed my lips, trying to prevent a grin. It didn't work. "Fine, you win."

He smacked his lips and moved closer. "But I can make the exception, I wouldn't want to ruin your perfect day that is filled with nothing to complain about."

"You're so considerate," I grumbled around another bite. He reached for the tools and I shook my head. "You don't really have to move them," I laughed. "I was only kidding!"

"No, no, what her royal highness wants, she will get."

I jabbed him in the ribs, before finally beginning to eat the innards of the sandwich.

"There," he said sweeping a hand across the table. "A royal place for your royal rump."

I choked. His hand slammed against my back. When I could breathe again, I scowled at him. "That was uncalled for."

"Not entirely," he grinned, once again pleased with himself. He took another bite of the sandwich, his Adam's apple bobbing. I would never admit it to him, but I always liked how it contoured his neck, and the way his nose was hooked and a little crooked. It was imperfect, like our friendship, but I liked him all the more for it.

Hopping up onto the spot he had cleared, I gestured with my chin toward the table. "So where is this one going?"

"Off to Salem," he said, running a hand over the wood. "Hopefully later today."

It looked finished to me, but who was I to judge. I'd tried before, but like most things, Roland was stubborn when he knew what he wanted. I liked that about him too—it was pleasant to know a friend wasn't fickle.

"Very neat, Mr. Bigshot."

He shrugged his shoulders and continued eating. Leaning back against his workbench, I couldn't help but notice how relaxed he was here. So at home. A pang of unease ran through me again. Something had been bothering me for weeks now, months, actually.

Ever since Kari's wedding I had felt displaced. Maybe it was the change in relationship with my best friend, or maybe it was this longing sense of restlessness, but I was frustrated. That's all I knew, frustration.

Looking at Roland and the ease with which he stood in his shop, I inhaled deeply—a little jealous. Maybe if I mustered up enough strength, I could relax like him.

"Guess what?" he asked, his mouth half-full.

"What?"

"I have another potential client for you."

I cocked my head to the side, snatching a barbecue-flavored chip from the open bag. "Another?"

He nodded. "She liked the 'quaint elegance' of my site." He held up a hand, "Her words, not mine."

I laughed. "Well, did you send her my information?"

"Just gave her your card. She was in here earlier this morning and when I told her you lived in town, she wanted to meet you."

"Oh," I said, a little taken aback. More often than not I conducted meetings with my clients over the phone. "Do you have her information?"

"She said she would get in touch with you."

I nodded, staring toward the end of his shop.

"What's wrong?"

I blinked, Roland was watching me, always seeing too much. Forcing a smile, I sighed. "I'm just a little distracted today. Umm, did you hear Mason is moving back later this week?"

Roland turned away. "Oh," he said softly, picking up the glasses he wore to protect his eyes. "That's good, maybe we can all get back together some night."

I nodded, annoyed at the lump that had formed in my throat. What was wrong with me these days? I hadn't seen Mason since Kari's wedding, but that didn't mean I hadn't spent more time looking at his online profiles than was healthy. Or that I hadn't risked sending a rather bold message to him two days ago.

"Yeah, maybe," I mumbled.

We'd never spoken about the night of Kari's wedding. Roland had been there for me, just like I had for him years ago. As though conjured from some ghost of a memory, I felt as though I could smell the smoke from a bonfire and hear the bullfrogs croaking in the pond near Joel's house. That night, during our last summer before college, Roland's carefree façade had broken. I still remembered laying on that worn trampoline with him, our shoulders touching as we gazed at the stars. He'd not said a word, and I hadn't either, but I had glanced over and saw a tear roll from the corner of his eye.

It had been enough to take my breath away. That was ten years ago, and we'd still never spoken about it.

Sometimes there were moments in life, cracks that were so deep that to even look at them again caused pain. They were the moments that transformed a person, moments when life becomes a bit too real and all the noise fades away to a steadying quiet of endless longing.

I'd felt it in Roland while we lay on that trampoline—the last night of summer coming to an end before we all left for college.

Looking his way now, I wondered what made Roland's brow furrow so deeply again. I nearly asked him what was wrong before Cole stepped into the workshop. "A Mrs. Kent is here?" He said it like a question, holding up a sticky note.

Roland waved toward me, "That's the lady."

"Oh," I blinked—the moment of revere shattered. Whatever glimpse I'd had into Roland was gone. Wiping my fingers on my jeans, I hopped off the table and grabbed my backpack. "Thanks for the sandwich, I owe you."

He smiled, the lines along his brow disappearing, "Don't you always?"

It was my turn to wink and I swung out the door to meet this new client.

CHAPTER 3

Her name was Kendra, Mrs. Kendra Kent and I liked her as soon as she called a cheery hello from across Roland's shop. She had a bright beaming smile that made her face glimmer with humor. But it was her cheerful, watchful eyes that added a timelessness to her countenance, forcing me to wonder at her age. I'd met many much younger than Mrs. Kent who'd had the life sucked from their eyes.

Mrs. Kent, it seemed, had forced life to abound in her joyful complexion.

I laughed as she finished another story about her husband who would be arriving from England any day now. According to her, Mr. Kent was the soul of generosity and she expected they would one day run out of money because he gave it away too quickly. She laughed and waved a hand, her mirth pouring forth a warmth that was greater than the steaming coffee mug pressed against my palms.

Smiling, I glanced down and picked at a napkin on the table. The clatter and familiar ambiance of Café Aroma's clientele further put me at ease. I grinned completely content, "And how long have you been married?"

"Would you believe it? Thirty-nine years next month." She clucked her tongue. "Who would have thought I would love spending so many years with one man." Laugh lines creased around her eyes and mouth, the best kind of wrinkles, hard-earned rewards for optimism.

"That's wonderful," I said.

"It is," she nodded, brushing a crumb off of her pale, blue blouse. The color was beautiful against the black tint of her skin. "That man has my heart, and he knows it."

The way she talked about Mr. Kent made me want to meet him. I hoped someday I would be like Mrs. Kent when talking about my husband.

A passing wisp of a dream with Mason ran through my mind. Taking a sip of coffee, I pushed the thought of his warm gaze aside.

Mrs. Kent sighed, looking outside the window for a fraction of a second before turning to me, her manner suddenly professional. "I guess we had better get on. Roland tells me you're the best in the business when it comes to this sort of web-thing."

It was my turn to laugh. "I don't know about the best, but I can certainly help."

"Don't be modest, I've seen his website and it's clean, easy to use, and made me stare at it for hours. But that was also because I wanted to buy everything Roland makes. Now, I've already told you about the Bed & Breakfast Mr. Kent and I have. So we want to get it up and online as soon as possible, but there are still some details that need to be completed."

I nodded. "Have you had anyone take pictures?"

"Oh," she said and ducked down to begin digging through her purse. After a few minutes of her bumbling with her phone, she handed it face up to me. "Scroll through those," she said, taking off the leopard print reading glasses to watch my expression.

Flicking through the photos, I could see this was more than a B&B. It was a haven. A recluse mansion tucked between two mountains in North Carolina, decorated with such a sense of both grandeur and quaint charm that I immediately wanted to explore. A few of the images had scaffolding or buckets of paint sitting in the corners.

"It's beautiful," I said. I could already picture the grand weddings and events this place could hold. What had seemed like a simple project by my estimation now grew in importance. "Did you build this?"

"No, it's one of those flip projects," she waved a hand in dismissal. "We hired a married couple to make it look this way. As you can see, they are nearly finished."

"That's wonderful," I took a deep breath. "Well, normally with a project like this, I like to see the finished work in person. I tend to be 'hands-on' when it comes to my work." Mrs. Kent smiled at that. "However, since this is in North Carolina, I don't know if my schedule will allow for me to travel there and back, plus that will increase the cost for you and your husband. One way to go around that is for you to hire a photographer when everything is ready. With those pictures, I will be able to build a look for your site, as well as content to entice future guests. And of course, we will have meetings to discuss just what kind of content you would like on your website."

Mrs. Kent nodded, "That sounds doable, but I do have one question for you. Have you ever been to England?"

It was a turn of conversation that I hadn't been expecting. "No."

"You must go."

"Perhaps after this job I will," I offered, smiling.

Mrs. Kent shook her head. "No, you misunderstand. What I mean is for this job you must go. Mr. Kent and I will pay for everything—but you must go."

I laughed, and then stopped when I realized she was perfectly serious. "I—I don't think, at least, I'm not sure if I will have the time."

"We always make time for what's important."

"I don't know if going to England is the most important thing for your Bed and Breakfast."

"Of course it is." Mrs. Kent said, not budging. "I want the guests who stay with us to feel as though they have traveled to England. Everything we have done has been to create this atmosphere and I want every detail to evoke the British countryside." She flipped through her pictures, showing me the carefully constructed English garden. She was right, everything looked as though it had stepped out of a BBC drama.

"How can you write and design a website for me if you've never been to England? Imagination can only take you so far. You did say you like a 'hands-on' approach."

I should have had an answer for her. So many times I had reasoned with clients, but the frankness with which Mrs. Kent spoke kept me from easing her mind with platitudes.

"Do you want to know why I asked Roland about you?" Mrs. Kent continued. "It was because of what I read on his site. Everything breathed a life I knew, and brought to mind my childhood." She reached down again and pulled a piece of folded paper from her purse. At a glance, I recognized a printed page from Roland's site, albeit, the colors slightly muted from poor ink.

"You wrote this," she said, pointing at the very words I had written, "and when I read it I could hear the cicadas on a summer's evening, the steaming heat of a cracked and worn parking lot, the beads of sweat dripping off a glass Coca-Cola bottle, and the glimmer of lightning bugs dancing in the night." She smiled, those lines appearing again, her eyes twinkling with memories.

I was touched that something I had written had evoked so much within her. "They're just words," I shrugged.

"No," she said, gently. "It's a breath of life that shows what makes Landing, Alabama—Landing, Alabama. These words, this place, are a part of who you are. I grew up in a town similar to this, and your words made me feel all of it again. It took me right back to childhood." She beamed. "And it was why I looked at Roland's work, which then, of course, spoke for itself."

"And then you came all this way to meet me?" I asked, uncertain as to why she would come so far.

She waved a hand, a familiar gesture. "No, my brother lives not far from here. I came to see him and thought I should stop by this little town. I wanted to meet Roland myself since I'd spent so much time on the phone with him, he's a sweetheart, isn't he?"

I laughed, "Yes, ma'am."

"And good looking too," she gave me a knowing look. "I knew he had a good voice on the phone, but I was not expecting him to look like that."

I smiled, making a mental note to tell Roland he had an admirer when I saw him next. It would be a challenge to see if I could embarrass him, but this just might do the trick. A smile lifted one side of my mouth just thinking about it. Anything to make Roland laugh was well worth the effort.

"But I am getting off-topic," Mrs. Kent said, "What I need is for you to write about my Bed & Breakfast the way you wrote about Roland's shop. I want the words to come from you, that you would know England the way I do. The essence of England needs to evoke passion and propriety, romance, and structure. It needs to have that feel of a timeless world that is now within reach. And the only way you can do that is to go there yourself. As I said, Mr. Kent and I will pay. Between you and me," she leaned forward conspiratorially, "money isn't an issue. But let's not tell Mr. Kent that." she winked and sat back with a satisfied grin.

An internal debate raged—excitement and uncertainty battling. The world of Jane Austen seemed to lay before me. Perhaps I could go and discover some peace to the unrest I'd recently been feeling. But wasn't that running away? Hadn't I promised myself that I wasn't going to run away anymore? My resolution wavered.

Glancing out the window, I bit my bottom lip in uncertainty. To step away sounded wonderful, glorious even, but was it responsible?

It didn't seem responsible, and I prided myself on being that way. A nagging feeling prodded me. Hadn't Charlotte Lucas always been the responsible one? Unlike Elizabeth Bennett, she hadn't had the privilege to choose.

But perhaps I did. Perhaps I could do this. My all too often abandoned sense of adventure perked.

"Don't give me your answer now, think about it, check your schedule, and then let me know." Mrs. Kent beamed again as the espresso machine behind the counter beeped.

I nodded.

"Now, tell me, how did you become such a web aficionado?"

After another hour of filling in Mrs. Kent on my life since college, we then parted ways. I had her contact information in my phone, and I was supposed to call her within the month to tell her my decision.

Back and forth I went, debating between the idea of going to England, or staying here. On the one hand, it seemed obvious I should go—for once my sense of adventure could be set free. But there was a reason for my hesitation and I knew who could help me with my problem.

Snatching up my phone, I sent a quick text to Roland. We would often take walks in the park in the evenings and tonight I needed one more than usual. Later when I was back in my apartment designing, the telltale beep chimed on my phone.

I glanced down, hoping it was Mason. He still hadn't given me an answer and it had been two days. Pursing my lips, I pushed back the fear that Mason had found me too forward, and opened Roland's message.

He could meet me at the park in fifteen minutes.

Saving my work, I threw on some leggings and a sweatshirt before hastening out the door.

CHAPTER 4

"I'm not sure I understand this debate." Roland was looking at me as though I had two heads.

"Maybe you aren't listening," I countered, breathless as we walked quickly along the paved pathway. "On the one hand, I could stay here and make sure everything gets done and—"

"And on the other hand," Roland butted in, "you could go on an all-expenses-paid trip to England. Tell me again why you needed to talk this out?"

"Because I need to be responsible."

"Responsible?" he scoffed.

"Yes, responsible. I have bills to pay, I have Chandler to take care of," I waved a hand back toward downtown as though we could see my six-year-old golden retriever. He should have come walking with us, but he was too lazy to traipse to the park, even though I'd tried more than a few times. Once he'd just sat there and refused to move. I'd had to call Roland and have him carry Chandler back to my loft. I still wasn't sure if I would ever live that embarrassment down.

"Oh please," Roland nudged my arm. "You're just making excuses and you know it. If this were me," he breathed as we rounded a curve along the path, "I would be on that plane tomorrow."

"Even though you have tons of orders to fulfill and a deadline for each of them?"

He paused, and opened his mouth, but then shut it again in thought.

"See, I knew it," I said, laughing, "you would have the same issues I'm having."

"No, not true. I was just coming up with my rebuttal." His laugh matched my own.

"Sure." I rolled my eyes.

"You have no idea how beautiful England is." He continued to encourage the idea. Roland's grandparents still lived in Scotland and he visited them at least once a year. Ever since he'd turned sixteen his mom had allowed him to travel overseas for visits. Many times, he'd filled my mind with pictures of the British countryside, it was one of my favorite things.

"As you've told me many times," I sighed, pushing loose strands of hair that had escaped from my ponytail away from my face. Roland enjoyed driving along the winding roads of Scotland, around the lochs, across the border, and through the English countryside. Over the years he'd explored much of the UK, alone or with his grandparents.

"When's you're next visit?" I asked.

"About a month."

"Oh, so soon?" I pursed my lips. Usually, he told me when he was planning to travel.

"Stay on subject, just take the job." His voice lowered, nearing on earnest. I peered up at him, curious. He was watching me, his eyes intense, I looked away, feeling the sudden change. "Dani, you've got to do this. You'll regret it if you don't."

My heavy ponytail swung along my neck as we pushed on. He was waiting for my answer, I could feel it.

"I told her I would think about it," I admitted.

"That's what I mean, what is there to think about?"

A few things came to mind. Mostly one prominent reason that I wouldn't voice—I was embarrassed to admit it even to myself. "Lots of things." Silence held between us for a few breaths.

"Sometimes I don't get you." He mumbled slightly under his breath, his deep voice stirring something inside me.

"You're no easy book to read either, Roland." That earned me a sidelong look, one I refused to return. "At least Mrs. Kent thinks you're easy on the eyes," I laughed.

"She said what?" He pretended to be offended.

"Oh yes, she told me you had a lovely voice and that she was pleased to see you were as handsome as you sounded."

The cold wind pushed past us, stinging my cheeks, but I didn't think that was the reason Roland's skin was flushed.

"She's a piece of work. Did you know she wants to be called Mrs. Kent rather than Kendra because she likes the way it sounds? She said she always wants to be reminded that she is married to her husband and that together they are a pair."

"Sounds like the two of you spent an inordinate amount of time on the phone together," I said, playfully. Roland chuckled. "That is kind of sweet, though," I admitted. I could hear Mrs. Kent saying that about her husband. She certainly doted on him. I smiled to myself, Mrs. Kent was a romantic at heart, we had that in common.

On we walked, and my phone buzzed a few times. I checked to make sure it wasn't Mason. The knot in my stomach where he was concerned was growing tighter by the minute. After a full lap with hardly anything said between us, I checked my phone one more time—worrying.

"Would you answer something honestly if I asked you?" Roland's voice broke into my thoughts. All humor had disappeared from his voice, replaced by a seriousness I had long avoided. His question pulled at me. It felt like standing at the edge of a deep lake and staring into the water, the depths unknown, yet the reflection familiar.

Roland always saw too much.

"Depends on what you ask," I said, slightly hesitant.

"I need to know if you're going to answer honestly first," he nudged my shoulder again; an attempt to make light of something serious.

"Didn't I tell you I was going to be honest this year? If I can't answer honestly, I just won't say anything."

"Fair enough," he nodded and we passed by a mother pushing her baby in a stroller. A sharp wind brushed by and I knew I was going to take a hot shower when I got home. It would feel glorious.

"Why didn't you go on that date with Alex?"

Of all the questions I had been expecting him to ask, that certainly wasn't one of them. Alex had asked me out just before Christmas. He was around my age, nice, steady job, handsome, but not my type. And that was the hard part—I didn't know how to explain why he wasn't my type.

"I thought I told you why."

"I wouldn't be asking if you had," Roland pointed out.

"Maybe you should talk to my mother," I said. "She's asked me nearly twenty times."

"And you told her what?"

I sighed. This was always the hard part with Roland. By some unspoken agreement, we usually avoided talking about relationships with each other. It was one of the reasons I so enjoyed spending time with him. With Roland, I didn't feel the pressure of emptiness, I didn't feel the longing to add something to a conversation when it came to talking about relationships or marriage, and I had hardly anything to offer. Like me, Roland was single. It was an understood point that we didn't talk about.

"I told her Alex wasn't my type and I wasn't interested in him." I sniffed; the cold air was making my nose run. Roland didn't answer and I had the distinct feeling he was digging for something.

I could meet him head-on. With Roland, I was a bolder version of myself. "You want to know, don't you?" I asked.

He glanced down but didn't meet my gaze. "Know what?"

"You want to know if I still have feelings for Mason." His name burned on my tongue.

Although Roland and I never really talked about relationships, he was able to easily read me when it came to Mason. It was one of my greatest fears, that others would see how much I wanted to be with Mason.

"Do you?" Roland kept his eyes focused forward.

I shrugged. "Yes."

He nodded, accepting that. "Have you ever told him?"

My heart pinched in dread. Did he know about the message that was currently waiting for a response? The one I had sent out of pure boldness that I was beginning to regret?

"Sort of."

"What do you mean by sort of?"

"I-I…I mean I try to when I see him. And we text and stuff every now and then."

"But you haven't actually said the words, or asked him out?"

I blanched. "I don't think I could ask him out." But that was rather close to what I'd already done.

"You could, it's easy. All you have to do is say the words," he glanced down at me and smiled. "I can help you learn how to say the phrase, *'My dearest, Mason, I've loved you since middle school, please be the love of my life.'*"

"Forget it," I shook my head, hating how he mocked, "you wouldn't understand."

"I wouldn't?"

"No," I said, my arms beginning to gesture before us. I tended to talk with my hands, especially when agitated. "You don't know what it's like to be in love with someone and never have them see you the way you long to be seen."

Roland didn't answer. His frustration was palpable and radiating off of him. It became like a wall between us. I wanted to bridge that gap, thinking that maybe if he saw the risks I did take, he would leave me alone.

"Besides," I said, "I have taken a chance. Two days ago, I offered to help Mason set up his website for when he moves his practice here. I know he plans to renovate the old barbershop. I want to help him build his online presence. And, you know, it will lay a groundwork for us to get to spend time together without the whole group there."

We continued and I waved to the Johnsons who walked by. They often had dinner at my parent's house on Friday nights.

"He's the real reason you won't go to England, isn't he?"

Roland's words cut straight to my heart.

It was the one thing I was most uncertain about and he had seen it. I took too long to answer and Roland stopped suddenly. I turned to him, questioning.

"You've got to get out of your head about him, Dani. He has no idea how you feel. Zero."

His words hit me as hard as a blow.

"That's harsh," I said, swallowing back the tears that were forming. I would not cry in front of Roland over this.

"Dani," his voice had softened, "I just think that you're giving up a lot for a distant hope."

My phone buzzed against my thigh, but I didn't pull it out. I was too busy trying to hold myself together. Of all the people in the world, Roland was the only one who could pull my walls apart so easily—and at times like this, I hated him for it.

"You're going to have to take a leap of faith sometime." His words were nearly a whisper.

I nodded. "I get it, I'm a coward." I began to back away.

"Dani, that's not what I meant."

"No, it's fine," I waved the words away. "I just, I've got some work to do, so I'll just," I hooked a thumb over my shoulder and hurried in that direction.

So much for not running away.

He caught up to me easily, his strides matching my own. Worry laced through my mind with every step. Maybe Roland was right. Maybe I had spent too much time hiding in the corners, in the shadows with disappointed hopes. Was it possible to be strong enough to boldly say what I wanted?

My door came in sight and I darted across the empty street—the lamps glowing with soft, yellow light.

"I'm sorry," Roland said, he was behind me as I pulled out my key and unlocked the door. "I didn't mean to upset you."

"You didn't, and it's fine," I shrugged. It was a lie, and I had promised to tell the truth. Roland knew it was a lie too. Again, my phone buzzed.

I pulled it out and read the words. Once, and then again. I smiled, my confidence bolstered, if only slightly.

Staring down at it, I whispered, "He said yes. We're going to meet next week." In five days to be exact.

"Good," Roland said, "well, goodnight."

"Goodnight." I looked up and caught a glimpse of Roland's expression before he turned away. He hadn't noticed, otherwise, he wouldn't have let me see it.

The disappointment and sadness there caught me off guard. It reminded me of the bonfire and that trampoline. Maybe someday I would ask him about that night, I wasn't the only one with secrets.

Distracted, I glanced at my phone again.

Maybe next week when I saw Mason, I could show Roland what I was made of. I would be bold, I would take that leap of faith he was talking about and tell Mason how I felt. Then I could ask Roland about the bonfire. Maybe he would tell me.

Long into the night I tossed and turned while trying to fall asleep, but every time I came close to drifting off, the image of Roland's sad eyes haunted me.

Getting up from my bed, I pulled back the curtains as Chandler nudged my leg with his wet nose. Across the rugged plaza of downtown, I spotted the yellow light glowing like a lightning bug on a warm summer evening from a window in Roland's shop.

It seemed he wasn't sleeping either.

CHAPTER 5

We are all idiots in love.

Charlotte Lucas said something to that effect in *Pride and Prejudice*…or maybe it was fools…I couldn't remember. Whatever it was, I understood the message. It was time I stopped being a fool and told Mason how I felt.

Placing a hand against my stomach I took a calming breath. I could do this—it was just words. Roland had encouraged me to take a leap of faith, and I would. I could show him my inner strength.

Leaning closer to the mirror, I put on my makeup like war paint, trying to instill some confidence. My favorite jeans and sweater became my armor.

The past week and a half had moved quicker than I thought. Mrs. Kent had messaged me twice, asking for my final answer, but I'd yet to send her one. Deep down I knew that tonight would be the defining factor—it all depended on Mason.

Biting my lip, I nodded at my reflection and avoided looking out the window of my loft where I knew I would see Roland's shop. Of course, we had spoken over the past week, but never about our argument. I didn't like it, the distance that had fallen between us—it was like we were skirting around the truth.

All-day my insides felt as though they were shaking, nearly trembling and they didn't stop even as I walked to the abandoned barbershop where I would meet Mason. I had planned to come right out with it. To tell him we should grab dinner and then maybe he would understand my feelings.

I was going to take that leap of faith. I could do it, and I would do it.

My strategy was thrown off track slightly when I arrived and found Mr. Martin inspecting the place, making measurements, and conversing with Mason about proposed renovations. I waited near the front door that was covered with dust, awkwardly adjusting my leather backpack on my shoulder as I waited. My fingers trembled as I held my phone and tried to instill some sense of calm back into my body.

It was nearly ten minutes before Mason made his way over to me smiling.

"Hey, thanks for coming!" He beamed. He had the beginnings of a beard growing along his jaw. I tried not to stare.

"Absolutely," I swallowed. "Is there somewhere we can get started?"

He glanced around, "Sure, here," he spun one of the old barber chairs around for me to sit in. The leather was cracked and torn in places. Not ideal, but I could manage.

Slipping into the chair, I busied myself with pulling out a notebook and pen. Mason took a seat and then got up again to answer a question from Mr. Martin. When he returned, his phone went off and he answered it before I could say a word. I waited patiently, my foot swinging back and forth as I twirled the pen between my fingers.

"Sorry," he said, slipping into the chair. "Too many things to think about."

"That's okay," I smiled, "I'm sure there's lots to do."

"Tons. I was just telling Mr. Martin that I want to resurrect some of the feel of this place. Everyone knows it's the barbershop, so let's keep some of its original vibe. I'm actually going to repurpose these chairs for the waiting room." He patted the chair he was sitting on. "Redone, of course, new leather cushions and all that."

"Neat," I said. "That's helpful, it gives me an idea of the style you're going for." I began writing on my notepad.

"Exactly," he said enthusiastically and began to launch into descriptions of what he was hoping his practice would look like. At one point he got up and began pointing out various areas for the reception desk, the partitions, the columns, and so on. I scribbled away, inspired by his enthusiasm.

With a few prodding questions, I started to get a feel for what he would need online. We talked of built-in scheduling capabilities, online appointment data systems, automated emails, search engine marketing, and search engine optimization. The more we talked, the more I began to realize that this project was going to take more of my time than I had predicted. Normally I didn't contribute to every detail, but for Mason, I was willing to go the extra mile.

The light outside began to dim and I suddenly realized two hours had passed.

"Well," I said, closing my notebook, "I think this gives me a great launching point. I can whip up a contract and have it sent your way." Pulling out my laptop, I named a price that was a steal for the amount of work I was going to do. Mason agreed almost immediately and I smiled as I scanned through my forms. I would have to change a lot of details.

"Can I send this to you tomorrow? I will need to add all of the specific details we discussed."

"Sure," he said, standing and stretching. "You're the best."

I bit back a smile, trying not to seem too eager. An email from Mrs. Kent appeared. Most likely it was her response to the preliminary contract I had sent her— no promises, just some outlined details. It would give her a chance to see everything visually and to make some suggestions of her own in the notes section.

"Are you hungry?" Mason asked, checking his watch. "It's later than I thought."

"Yeah," I said, my voice a little higher than normal. I hopped off the chair, tucking away my things, and followed him out into the cool night. Mrs. Kent could wait.

Walking lighter than I had since my argument with Roland, I asked Mason about his move. He told me all about his trip and some problem with the movers as we reached Fine Eatery, a southern home-cookin' restaurant on the edge of downtown Landing.

The waitress brought our food, and I smiled to myself as Mason dug in enthusiastically. That was something about Mason. He always did things with such passion and assertiveness. At times, I could tell other people found him abrasive, but I never did.

My nerves began to get the better of me and I knew I would have to tell Mason how I felt before it was too late. I had planned to ask him to dinner, but we were already eating together. Glancing around the room as though I might find refuge, I took a deep breath. I wondered if Mason could feel the tension, only to find him happily eating and commenting on how good the food was.

"They don't make stuff like this anywhere outside of Landing," he shook his head again, as if in disbelief.

"Mason?" I asked, my fork held awkwardly in my hand.

"Yeah?" He took another huge forkful of chicken pot pie.

"I wanted to ask you something," I swallowed, "or tell you something." Blood was pounding heavily in my ears. I hated feeling like this.

"Yeah?" he said again, slightly distracted.

I opened my mouth to speak when his phone rang. I cursed my luck.

The phone flew to his ear, "Hey!" he said, smiling. "Sorry," he mouthed to me.

I waved a hand as though it was no problem and began to stare at my plate, I'd hardly touched it. His words were casual, heightened with laughter as they nearly always were. Biting back my fear, my eyes fell upon my glass of water and the beads of perspiration dripping down the sides. I suddenly felt too hot in my sweater.

"No, I get it," Mason said, "it's frustrating for sure. Yeah…well no, that's not true. I'm sure they won't break all of your things." Whoever was on the other side of Mason's phone had a lot to say. Though I couldn't hear the other voice, a sudden wondering began to stir in my heart—a little prick of trepidation.

"Don't worry about it," Mason said calmly. He leaned forward on the table. "Just be safe on your drive down here tomorrow."

Everything inside me went cold. I wanted to shake away those words because I knew exactly where this was headed.

"Yeah, okay," Mason said, and as much as I wanted to tune him out, there was nowhere for me to go. Instead, I remained fixated on that stupid glass of water. "Okay, I'll talk to you tomorrow. Let me know when you leave…yeah…yeah…love you too." He hung up, putting his phone back into his pocket.

"Girlfriend," he said in apologetic explanation. "She's moving down here with me. I'm excited for her to meet everyone."

"Oh," was all I could say—it was the only word I could think. Blood was pumping through my ears as pieces of me were threatening to tear apart.

"You might have met her, actually," he said, "she was at Kari's wedding. She caught the bouquet. Her name's Nancy." Flashes of that night flew through my mind. I'd seen it—how could I have been so stupid as to hope?

"That's great," I said, forcing myself to smile and not break. This is what it felt like to drown and have no one hear you. I was screaming at the top of my lungs, but no one could tell.

I had thought he was single. Could have sworn he was.

After Kari's wedding, I had kept a close eye on social media, searching for any hint that he was in a relationship. But there had been nothing. No clue, no hint. Nothing.

But I'd seen something between him and this Nancy that night of the wedding. I was an idiot to think I could ever have him.

Charlotte Lucas was right. I was a fool in love.

Nothing but a fool.

CHAPTER 6

Turns out it was a pretty quick process to break the heart. All it took was a few words. Some nonchalance, a little unawareness, and it could shatter.

I would have thought I'd be used to it by now, but the very breath seemed almost sucked from my lungs at Mason's words.

The bell on Fine Eatery's door clanged.

As though from outside my body I heard someone yell Mason's name and come over to our table. I heard my name too and smiled in welcome as some of our high school friends slapped Mason on the back, hugging him and welcoming him home. Kari said hi to me, her fingers laced through Joel's. Everything a blur.

I felt eyes on me and saw Roland in the group. One glance was all it took, his brow furrowed and I nearly flinched. Looking away quickly, I tried to hide the shattered pieces of my heart—he always saw too much.

Blinking, I took a sip of water just to have something to do. There were voices all around me and before I could even think straight, additional tables were pulled toward ours. I nearly laughed at the absurdity of it all.

Stuffing all emotion, all thought down, I forced myself to interact with everyone. I listened as they ordered, as they talked to Mason about his practice. I refused to even frown as Mason talked

about Nancy, but the one thing I wouldn't do is I wouldn't look at Roland again. He was on the opposite side, at the end of our long, makeshift table and I felt his eyes on me like a weighted blanket. I knew if I looked at him, he would see all of it—and I couldn't do that, not yet.

Dinner dragged on and before too long I checked my phone. There was that unread email from Mrs. Kent blinking at me.

As though suddenly clear, I knew what I needed to do. Resolution or not, I needed to go.

Making my excuses, I left the table, telling Mason I would send him the contract as soon as I was finished. He nodded and told me thanks, but was immediately captured by a question from Kari.

I nearly ran from the restaurant.

Icy, winter air cut through my sweater. For late February it was unseasonably cold—but I welcomed it, focusing on it. Anything to keep the pieces together until I got home.

As I crossed the road and passed through the plaza, I heard someone call my name. I groaned, knowing just who it was. I could hear him running.

"Dani!" he called again, and I stopped, stealing myself for what I would see. I turned just as Roland was crossing the road and reaching the small plaza of downtown Landing. His dark hair was pushed back in the wind as he ran, and I could tell he was breathing heavily. He must have taken some time to slip away, clearly having sprinted to reach me.

"Hey," I said, forcing a smile as he slowed and stopped before me. I glanced at him for just a moment and then looked away. I could feel the pieces beginning to tear apart.

"Don't do that," Roland said, his deep voice soft and warm—like a hug.

"Do what?" I shrugged, still not looking at him.

"Don't try and pretend like everything is okay." He moved closer and my breath hitched. This was too much, I didn't want him to see me like this.

"Not pretending," I managed, and finally met his gaze. His eyes, so dark they were almost black, were kindled with warm concern. "I'm fine." I swallowed.

"Dani," he murmured, and I suddenly feared he was going to pull me into a hug. I couldn't let that happen, I just couldn't. He brushed his hand along my arm. I pulled back, not wanting to break in front of him, ready to flee.

His hand hung awkwardly between us before he tucked it away in his pocket.

"I'll be fine," I sniffed and wiped at my nose with my sleeve. Tears were beginning to form in my eyes. I needed to leave. "You can go back, I'll be fine." I tightened my jaw, forcing my will to not bend. He hesitated and took a step closer, but I moved back. "It's fine, I have some work to finish. I-I-I will just do that."

Spinning on my heel, I ran the rest of the way home. Roland didn't call after me, and I wouldn't think of the hurt and pity in his eyes. I couldn't.

When I finally reached my loft, my collapse at the edge of my bed was worthy of a Disney princess, though not as graceful. I cried, the tears streaming down my face, which were only made worse when Chandler came and placed his head on the mattress next to mine.

How long I cried, I wasn't sure, but as the gasping stopped and I lay there on the floor staring at my ceiling, I suddenly knew it was all over. The foolishness of this pinning was done. No more.

Grabbing for my bag, I pulled out my laptop. The bright light from the screen nearly blinded me. Searching, I found the email from Mrs. Kent and the details she outlined. Checking the notes, I spotted one specific request. She wanted me to tour Highclere Castle. I didn't know much about it, only that it was where *Downton Abbey* had been filmed.

Glancing at the time, it was later than I thought. On a whim, I wondered if she was still awake and sent her a text. I received a call and warmed at the sound of her cheerful voice. My own sounded terrible and I lied, telling her I had a cold.

That didn't stop her from outlining details, and before I knew what was happening, we had an electronic contract signed with the agreement that all expenses would be billed to the Kent's. I got off the phone with inspiration and intent.

Hours later, I had my ticket, my passport, and my car packed. With the airport several hours down the road, I would need to get going. Glancing at the clock, the number three flashed at me. Arrangements were made and I was out the door.

As I started my engine, I glanced at my phone. There was only one unopened text message from Roland.

It read:

Here if you need me.

Typing, I sent him a message and then turned on some music before leaving it all behind and pulling away. I wondered what Roland would think when he read that message, maybe he wouldn't think I was a coward for running away, I certainly felt like one. The words I'd sent ran through my mind.

I'm taking Mrs. Kent's offer. Be back in a few weeks. My mom is getting Chandler in the morning, can you help her get him in the car? You know how lazy he is. Thanks.

Roland would help, I knew he would. As the lights of Landing drifted away in my rearview mirror, I decided to put it all behind me.

I was going to England.

CHAPTER 7

In my twenty-seven years, I'd probably read *Pride and Prejudice* at least five times, but it was the movie version with Kiera Knightley that I'd seen over and over again. It was that one movie that put a smile on my face and warmed me to my soul.

For years, I had wondered what made Charlotte Lucas give up. What had made her decide to marry Mr. Collins and leave her home? As I drove through the night, I pondered that scene when she tells Elizabeth she's going to marry Mr. Collins, a man who is ridiculous and unromantic. For the first time, I truly began to understand what she meant when she said she was frightened.

I was frightened. Scared that I would forever be alone, overlooked, and always uncertain. Terrified that a life of adventure, a life of living out my dreams, would forever be out of reach.

Pieces of me were just like Charlotte. She was pleasant and amusing, but not the leading lady. Too often I felt like the side character in my own life, as though I was the supporting role to some greater play going on.

I'd had enough. Maybe that's what this trip was all about.

I had the excuse of work, the contract to prove Mrs. Kent's desire for me to visit England, but what I didn't have was any real explanation for why it was so sudden. At least, not one I could share.

Anna had called while I was on the road. My text must have sounded desperate. I knew she could hear the emotion in my voice, the hurt. She didn't ask for all the details, and she didn't have to. In many ways, we understood one another. Hurts and struggles had bonded us over the years, this was nothing new—only painful.

I would get through it, I just needed space. Anna understood that more than anyone.

Hanging up, I arrived at the airport and hurriedly wiped away the remains of my tears. Fixing my makeup in the poorly lit bathroom, I grabbed a coffee and then found a secluded chair and Facetimed my mother. I always Facetimed her, just in case my dad was there too. He was deaf and if he was nearby, we always signed while we spoke so he could participate.

It was a quick conversation, and she was thrilled for me. I didn't have an answer for why I had left so suddenly, but she didn't press the matter. That was one thing I loved about my parents; they knew I would tell them when I could.

After two connecting flights, I finally landed in London. Time had lost its meaning. All I knew was the sun was up and it was cold. Slinging my hiking backpack—which doubled as my suitcase—over my shoulders, I made my way onto a bus and to the nearest hotel. It might as well have been America with its modern rooms, but no matter, tomorrow I would begin my journey to Highclere Castle.

As I researched, my travel, I found a bus that would take me to the closest town to the castle. From there I could take a taxi and then walk the rest of the way. A walk I didn't mind. In fact, in this weather, it would be welcoming.

Slapping my laptop shut, I slid beneath the covers and welcomed the sleep that enveloped me. Tomorrow I would explore a castle. Think of something Anna said.

Perfect. The thought was a curse.

I had made my way to Newbury, a town not far from Highclere castle only to see the dates on a little pamphlet the hotel clerk had given me. The castle was closed this time of year.

What was I going to do?

I'd traveled from Landing, Alabama without even seeing if the castle was open. I felt like a complete idiot. Why hadn't I thought to check?

Shoving that thought aside, I pushed back my annoyance. Maybe it said something of my being American, but I had simply expected the castle to be open.

The weather here was different than what I was used to—colder, harsher, but in a refreshing way.

Even the light outside was different. After a slow morning in London, I figured out the public transportation to get to Newbury. I'd been surprised looking at the sky, it was only 2:00 in the afternoon and already I could tell it would be dark before 5:00.

This was why I should have done more research before leaving. The only thing I had going for me was the lack of pressure when it came to time. Mrs. Kent was an easy client and she hadn't given me a timeline.

After locating my room in the quaint hotel, I left my things and started to explore Newbury. More than once I found myself checking my phone out of habit. Without WIFI, I wouldn't be able to talk to anyone. It's what I had wanted, some privacy and distance. Idly, I wondered what my parents were doing, what Roland was doing.

Checking the clock, I subtracted five hours. Most likely Roland was working in his shop—although that was a fair guess for most times of the day, even nights.

The food at a local pub was excellent and as I sat there listening to the chatter, I began to relax. I'd had enough of the pitying thoughts. So what if the castle wasn't open? According to the pamphlet, there were public walking paths. I could at least see the house exterior.

After talking to my waiter, I had a general idea of where I needed to go to get a taxi for the following day. Mrs. Kent wanted me to get a feel for England, and I would do the best I could.

Having a plan made me feel better. When I reached my room later that night, I sunk onto the bed and finally opened my notifications. There weren't as many as I was expecting. A couple of emails from clients, an email from Mrs. Kent about a place to eat, and three messages. Two from Roland and one from Mason.

I opened Mason's first.

> Heard you're out of the country for a client. I didn't realize I was working with a worldwide designer...jk...I know you're great at what you do. Have fun. We'll talk details when you get back.

I wanted to smile at his words, but that ache in my chest hadn't eased. Taking a deep breath, held the air in my lungs for a moment. I was done crying for Mason. He wasn't for me. I had to get that through my head.

The other messages were from Roland.

```
Have a great trip! Chandler is at your parent's house. Take time
to enjoy yourself.
```

And then:

```
Remember that time we got that frisbee stuck on the Johnson's
roof? Well, he finally noticed. Saw him taking it off yesterday.
It's only been 3 years. Anyways, had to tell you. Might give you
a laugh. I actually hope you don't see this until you get back.
Enjoy yourself.
```

Biting my lip, I dropped my phone onto the bed. Seeing Roland's messages only made me think of the look in his eyes when I left. It seemed like weeks ago, and yet, it was still raw.

At that moment I'd seen the pain and helplessness. Not pain I had caused, but empathetic pain for what I was going through.

By force, I managed to get a long night of sleep and was up early to rent a car, and drive to the walking trail that would give me a view of Highclere Castle. It was called Beacon Hill, and after a climb, I stood near the top as the yellow glow of a groggy sun rose further from the horizon. Turning in nearly a full circle, I saw no castle. Confused, I wondered if I had it all wrong.

A man and his dog walked up the trail to me. He smiled a gap-toothed grin and walked on. I wondered if I should follow him, but didn't want to get too close. Instead, I waited, taking a deep breath of air.

I'd thought the morning was silent—it was anything but quiet. Out on that hill, there was a sort of symphony of its own. Birds chirping, the winter wind whipping across the brown grass. Pieces of my dark hair tickled my neck as I took a deep breath. Out here, I could breathe.

Not wanting to move just yet, I sat down near the top of the hill and decided to listen as the English countryside greeted the day. Looking at the land before me, I could imagine what it must be like to ride a thundering horse over the fields. It must be a wondrous experience.

Was this what Mrs. Kent had wanted? Had she wanted me to experience the British countryside in all its beauty?

The far-off murmur of approaching voices reached me. I glanced over my shoulder and spotted a family making their way up the hill, all of them carrying backpacks, scarves covering their mouths, and wearing sunglasses. They looked like they were on an Everest expedition.

"We there?" the youngest child asked, a girl just reaching her teen years.

"Yeah," the father said. "It's right there."

"I don't see it," said the teenage boy.

"Look toward the trees, no further back. Here, line up with my arm. Right there, where my finger is pointing."

I glanced back toward the man and saw I had been facing slightly the wrong way. I looked toward the left where he was pointing. Peering, and squinting, I suddenly saw it. The top of the castle was just visible through the trees.

A laugh escaped my lips. So much for views of the castle. The roof was barely visible!

I listened as the family talked about it, and then they passed on without glancing my way. Staring in wonder, I suddenly remembered what my waiter had said the night before. This was probably the closest I would get to the house when it wasn't open for guests. Disappointment lingered.

Biting my lip, I worried away the sense of urgency that lingered. I could choose to make the best of this. And I would.

For the first time in a long time, I realized that no one was waiting for me for anything. No one could get in touch with me out here, and that thought was freeing. Leaning back, a cold wind stung my cheeks as the sun broke through the clouds. It warmed my face, my black winter coat absorbing its rays. I could get used to this.

After sitting there for what felt like hours, I rose to my feet, my knees cracking. With one last peek at the castle, I worked my way down the hill, passing groups of people as they began their climb. I climbed into my rented car and drove back to Newbury, only making one wrong turn where I managed to shift to the wrong side of the road for a moment. Luckily a car in the distance reminded me that the left side was correct.

That night, I emailed Mrs. Kent and told her about my problem. I tried to sound as positive as possible, in all reality, I had enjoyed my day, but it was a bit lacking. I had hoped to at least get pictures of the castle, but maybe a speck of roof would suffice. Laughing at my sarcasm, I was glad I could still amuse myself.

Pressing send on the email, I curled up on the bed and searched for things to do in Newbury. A local museum might be the answer to some of my problems. Maybe it would help me get a grasp for the style of Highclere Castle, then I would be able to word the Kent's site the way she wanted.

Settling in for the night, I began to design a draft for the Bed & Breakfast. After working with the colors, and look of the site, I stared at the blinking cursor, waiting for the words to come. Nothing did.

Perhaps tomorrow I would get a better idea of what to say.

Glancing at my messages, there was nothing new. I pursed my lips and sent a message to the family group text—only now realizing I hadn't even taken a picture. I promised to send one tomorrow.

Is it wonderful there?!

It was Anna.

It's different, still figuring things out. I may be a little unprepared. But I'll make the most of it.

I'm sure you will.

What Anna didn't know was my uncertainty on how to do just that. Suddenly, I realized just how far away I was. How different my life was from hers.

While I was always running, and seeking the very things I'd always wanted, Anna had them. We lived in two completely different worlds. Hers was set on a solid foundation of her family. That in no way made it easy, but it did have a semblance of order. I could no more easily understand the pressures of her day to day than she could understand the empty loneliness of having to do everything on my own.

Tears pricked my eyes as I readied myself for a confession.

> I think this trip was a mistake.
>
> *How come?*
>
> I'm realizing how lonely I am. No distance can fix that.
>
> *I mean...in many ways you're right.*

I blinked back the tears that were threatening to spill over. This brokenness inside was such a weakness of mine—a weariness of having to keep going, having to keep putting on a positive outlook. After a while, it became too much and what remained was a hollowness that couldn't be filled. At least not easily.

Anna continued typing.

> *Take it one day at a time. I'm here for you when needed.*
>
> I know. And thank you for that.
>
> *But it's not the same is it?*

Her questions were always so pure, so raw. Taking a shaky breath, I confessed my frustration.

> No. And it doesn't matter what I do during the day or how many friends I have, the truth of the matter is I'm on my own, and at times it can be really lonely.
>
> *I'm sorry.*
>
> Not your fault.
>
> *I wish there was more I could do. But here's what I think...you're going to have to figure out how to be okay with this on your own. No person can*

fill that void. You have to come to a place where you are okay with life the way it is. Accept it.

The tears flowed freely. Her words baring the very things I'd been struggling with. How did a person come to terms with the way their life had turned out? How could I accept my life for the way it was? How could I find joy in it?

When my breath settled, I found new purpose and determination, I could do this. I would do this.

`I'll try.`

She responded with a heart and I tossed my phone aside, only to remember I had never responded to Roland's message. Hovering my fingers over the keys, I searched for the right words—hoping he would respond.

`Hey! Thanks for helping my mom with Chandler…I appreciate it! Did he behave? And I do remember that frisbee. You should be a better catcher!`

I went back to work, experimenting with colors and the design of buttons for the top of the website. A responding email from Mrs. Kent came in. She seemed unfazed about Highclere Castle being closed and I had the sudden notion that she may have known about its open seasons all along. She was an interesting woman.

My phone dinged. It was Roland.

`Well…let's just say that was the worst throw known to mankind.`

A second later, my phone beeped again.

`Chandler made me pick him up. Big shocker there.`

I laughed at that.

`Why am I not surprised?`

```
I think he was pouting.

Oh, I'm sure he was!

How's England?
```

I paused, not sure how to answer that. What could I tell him? After my dramatic flight into the night, I had hoped for something more dynamic, more life-changing. There was that sense of adventure buried deep within that wanted to spread its wings.

I'd read a book once about a girl who felt like a bird trapped in a cage. Sometimes, I felt that too. But the only difference was I had built the cage around myself. No one had told me to fall for Mason. I had done that all on my own. And the cage door was open, but I was too afraid to fly.

```
It's different.

How so?

Just is…kinda hard to explain. I'll tell you when I get back.

When will that be?

I don't know yet. I'm kinda doing all of this on a whim.
```

I paused again, uncertain.

```
I know. That's good though. Let yourself take a break and go have
an adventure!
```

I didn't have the heart to tell him I was sitting alone in a hotel room with my laptop. Not much had changed from my loft.

```
Yeah. I will. Thanks again for helping my mom. I'm sure she
appreciated it.
```

```
Always, Dani.
```

I smiled at the nickname. He was the only one who called me that—or at least the only one allowed to. It'd been years ago at my college orientation that I'd been paired with a boy for some, 'introduce yourself' humiliation. I'd said my name, and he'd said his—I couldn't remember it now. But I did remember him asking me if I ever went by Dani.

I'd lied and said, "No."

Even now, so many years later, I wondered why I hadn't let that boy call me Dani. Maybe because Roland always had. And knowing Roland, he always would.

That thought pushed me off designing the website and down to the lobby to get more information for tomorrow. Anna had told me to figure out how to be okay on my own—and I would do it. I would go on an adventure if it was the last thing I did, if not for me specifically, then to at least have something to tell Roland when I got back.

CHAPTER 8

Newbury was a charming place. That was what I had decided as I spent two days exploring the town and popping in and out of museums and shops. I was determined to make the most of it.

I was in England. Me. Danielle Winthers was in England and it didn't matter if the sky was overcast and dreary, I was choosing to enjoy my time.

Having never watched *Downton Abbey*, I was at a loss to fully understand what importance Highclere Castle held. Perhaps it was like Pemberley. The great home of some man who seemed prideful, but was just shy and uncertain. Thinking of Mr. Darcy, I smiled to myself and peered across the English Countryside once more.

I could almost picture a Mr. Darcy of the Regency Era walking across the fields. I laughed and then stopped abruptly when I realized I was no longer alone. On my third morning in England, I had decided to return to Beacon Hill. This time the sky was overcast and there was no warmth on the horizon, but I didn't mind. The very air I breathed tasted of adventure.

Or at least that's what I told myself.

Nearly snorting at the thought, I held it back. There was a middle-aged woman with two dogs sitting on the hill about twenty yards from me. I knew she had heard my laugh and sent me an odd look. I had realized in the past few days that aside from a few short conversations in pubs or at the museums, I hadn't truly spoken to anyone. And my little introvert self was rather enjoying it.

I wasn't sure what that said about me, but it certainly couldn't be bad. Maybe it made me like Charlotte Lucas. I remembered the way she so enjoyed her little parlor. It was her place, a room to call her own.

Maybe that's part of what I was looking for—a place to call my own.

An hour later, I was standing outside a barn and watching as an enormous horse was led toward me. The tour guide was giving instructions to our group and as I swung into the saddle with a little help, I checked to make sure my phone was safely secured in my pocket.

Mrs. Kent had sent me an email the night before in response to my preliminary ideas for the website. Her feelings were the same as mine. The site didn't have the feeling of rest and relaxation—it didn't evoke peace.

I was determined to get a better grasp of what drew Mrs. Kent to England, and what pulled at my own heart. Over the last few days, I had felt something change. There was an essence here that was endearing to me and I was determined to seek it out, to define it.

As though in response to my thoughts, my horse shifted his weight. I leaned to the other side, my heart pounding as it always did when I rode a horse. Growing up, I'd ridden plenty of horses and spent hours in the saddle. Whether at a walk, a canter, or gallop, it was one of my favorite pastimes as a child. I wondered now why I had given it up.

My horse shifted again as the tour guide walked by.

"Easy Beardsley," he patted my horse's neck.

I stared. *Beardsley?*

What an odd name for a horse, and yet, I kind of liked it. It made me think of a butler with a heightened sense of importance. And with the way Beardsley was currently refusing to face any of the other horses I had a feeling he might live up to his name.

Nearby was the family I had overheard on Beacon Hill during my first morning in Newbury. Whether or not they recognized me, they didn't say. We all took time to introduce ourselves and I tried to remember names, but as usual, if I didn't say the name quickly, I lost it. And so, off we started on our tour, and I was at the back of a pack of essential strangers.

At least I knew Beardsley. As though he could hear me, I patted his bobbing neck.

Every now and then we stopped and the tour guide would point out various landmarks, his hands sweeping in gestures as his grey mare bowed her head to pick at some grass. I was amused that all of the horses in our group of ten seemed to take any chance they could to eat, but not Beardsley. No, he was a cut above the rest—a soldier maintaining his rigid posture.

We came to an open field and paced along a worn path near a stone wall. I wondered how long that fence had been there as we moved at a sedated pace. I idly remembered Roland telling me he couldn't stand horseback tours for this very reason. His comment had only prompted me to make fun of his driving. For all the calmness Roland had, he had one streak of adventure that I had never fully seen. He liked to ride fast.

Once, he'd told me about horseback riding in Scotland with his grandparents. Of course, he'd told me he was a kid at the time, but he'd said that he liked to give the horse free rein to thunder across the ground.

Nothing could be more opposite from the pace we were holding. It was the very essence of plodding. At that moment, I was quite jealous of young Roland.

"There it is," the tour guide yelled back and pointed into the distance with feigned enthusiasm.

Phones were pulled out and a few of the women exclaimed, "It looks just like it!"

From my spot at the back, I had to wait until the trees finally broke, and then, there it was—Highclere Castle. Those ladies were right, it did look exactly like the brochures. From our vantage point, it was more than likely a quarter of a mile away, but at least it was closer than Beacon Hill. As Beardsley came to a stop, I snapped a few pictures of the castle—realizing it was just a house. A grand house.

We moved forward a little further and then our tour guide encouraged us to dismount and walk the grounds. We could walk as far as a stone fence.

After staring at the castle for a few minutes, I confirmed my suspicions. From everything Mrs. Kent had talked about, this was not the feeling she was going for. Of course, the stately home was grand, expansive, and powerful, but to me, it didn't ignite my senses. It wasn't the doorway to retreat. It was grandeur, but not peaceful.

Pursing my lips, I walked back to Beardsley and snapped an up-close picture of him. "Portrait mode does wonders for you too," I murmured and rubbed his snout.

"Would you like me to take your picture?" Our tour guide asked, making me turn. I couldn't remember his name but figured I could manage.

"Please," I said and handed him my phone. I turned to fully face him and placed my hand under Beardsley's heavy head. Smiling I waited, only to realize the man wasn't lifting the phone and was instead staring at me in confusion. My smile faltered.

"Oh," he said, his brow clearing, "you want a picture with Beardsley?"

"Yes." Only then did I realize that most tourists would ask for a picture of the castle. A small wave of embarrassment rushed over me. "I'd like one with Beardsley first, then if you don't mind, would you take one with the castle?"

"Of course," he grinned, his blonde hair lifting in the wind that was picking up its strength by the minute.

To now take not one, but two pictures before this stranger was incredibly awkward. I smiled, trying to hide my embarrassment, and reminded myself that I could delete the image later if needed. Even as I thought it, I knew I wouldn't. Pictures were like time capsules, and how else would I explain what I did to my parents when I got back? And to Roland for that matter. I knew he would ask.

After enduring another fifteen minutes of the rest of the group taking pictures, the tour guide helped each of us back into the saddle before leading us along the path and back to the barn. I said goodbye to Beardsley, who still didn't seem to care about me, and went back to my hotel. Flicking through the photos from the day, I tried to use them as inspiration for Mrs. Kent's vision.

But it was not to be. No matter what I did, Highclere was simply not the right aesthetic.

As the pictures from the day uploaded to my computer, I spotted the one with Beardsley. Even though I could see the lines of hesitation in my eyes, I liked it. It was made all the better by the fact that Beardsley wasn't looking at the camera, or even acknowledging my presence. He was staring off into the distance like a prized stallion.

I laughed and scrolled through the rest of the images. Perhaps with the photos I had taken in Newbury, from the fields, and Beacon Hill, I would have enough to go off of. As I experimented, I began to work in a groove and the hours slipped past.

Long into the night I worked, and only when my eyes were hurting, did I save everything and close it down for the night. Maybe this was enough progress, or maybe not. However, there was one thing I was certain of, and it was that Newbury had nothing more to offer my project.

The only other place I could think of that would offer more inspiration was Chatsworth. It was the house that I knew was used as the location of Pemberley for the 2005 *Pride & Prejudice* adaptation. I wondered if it would even be worth the drive.

Resorting to some more last-minute research, I found that this house was closed as well. Disappointment welled in me—I'd come so far and yet, it seemed as though I had only scratched the surface.

Maybe I had been foolish to think I could run away from everything at home. My heart was tender, a little cracked in the wake of disappointed hopes. At some point, I would have to pick myself back up—I would have to face Mason again.

Oh, how thankful I was that I hadn't said anything to him. That could have been incredibly embarrassing—it was mortifying enough knowing that Roland was aware of my feelings.

Perhaps, it was time I go back home. Maybe this whole thing had been a ridiculous whim. A way for me to fix Roland's accusation that I never took any risks. That I was simply trying to force myself to be happy, to be "unstuck."

So far it hadn't worked. Here I was, the same Danielle, and I didn't have a plan. I'd been in England for less than a week on my own and only had a few pictures to show for it.

Maybe my time in England was done. The thought was at once comforting and disappointing.

Not wanting to make any rash decisions, I decided to sleep on it and make plans the following morning. It was the last thought I had before sleep took me.

Upon the morning, nothing had changed and I packed my bags for home.

CHAPTER 9

"What do you mean there aren't any more flights?" I asked the woman behind the counter. She wore a blue blazer and was doing a rather wonderful job of not making eye contact.

"It means that due to the incoming blizzard, no flights will be departing."

I had heard as much from the intercom announcements, but over the buzz of confusion in the airport, I couldn't believe it was true.

"I thought that wasn't for five more hours?" a man said over my shoulder to the woman. I leaned away from him as he pointed up at the tv screen near the desk. It was playing a minute-by-minute forecast and I couldn't help noticing he was right.

The woman huffed and smiled too sweetly at the man, but I cut her off before she could respond. I'd been on the other side of that counter before. Sometimes maintaining the protocol of a decision that someone high up put in place, was difficult.

"So, what are my options?" I asked.

The woman seemed gratified to not continue the conversation with the pushy man behind me. "Well, we can get in touch with you as soon as your flight is ready, but you should then remain inside the airport."

"And if I don't want to do that?"

"We can cancel your ticket and give you a credit to be used at a later date."

"That's fine," I said.

Her hands flew across the keys and I had little time to decide what I was going to do when she handed my card and ticket back to me. I gave her my thanks and turned away from the desk.

There was an odd sense of impending doom in my gut, or at least the restraint of freedom coming. Glancing back at the television mounted high on the wall, I watched the images scroll across the map. Snow, and lots of it, was coming.

I nearly laughed—my little southern body wasn't going to know what to do with hordes of snow.

Figuring my best option would be to rent a car, I traipsed back toward the car rental place with the distinct feeling of having already done this before. In some small way, I was gratified to be staying in England a bit longer, the unknown stretching before me. It was both wonderful and daunting at the same time.

Would I take this postponement as a gift or a curse?

Thinking of Roland, I knew I needed to look at this in a positive light and see if there was something else I could do to change my situation. Perhaps this would be the beginning of a new adventure.

Glancing to my left as I walked, I spotted the back of a rather tall, broad-shouldered man. He had hair just like Roland's—dark waves pushed back as though fingers had been run through it recently. The man was even wearing a jacket just like Roland's. I smiled to myself as a pang of homesickness washed over me.

I missed my friend. Though I was still uncertain what I would say to him. We hadn't spoken, at least not face to face, since my abrupt departure, but I was sure we could think of something.

The man turned and I stopped in my tracks. It was Roland.

Either it was him or some twin I had never known about. That hooked nose of his was too unique.

I stood there staring. "Roland?"

He turned fully toward me, blinked, and broke into a wide grin, the lines along the sides of his mouth deepening. It was a smile I knew so well. I couldn't help but laugh and hurry toward him. Throwing my arms around his neck, he pulled me close.

"Well, look at you, world traveler!" He beamed, letting me go to look me up and down. I felt as though the clouds of life had parted and sunshine was breaking through to warm me. He was all things light and comfort and until now I hadn't realized how much I had missed it.

With only a week since seeing him, I wondered why it affected me so much. "And look at you!" I smiled up into his eyes and then suddenly grew confused. "Wait, what are you doing here?"

He sighed. "I found cheaper flights to visit my Nan and Pap and so I thought I would leave early, only," he ducked his head to look out the expansive windows on the other side of the airport, "it seems the weather isn't going to cooperate…at least not for a few days."

"Oh," I said. "Why didn't you tell me?"

"I didn't want to mess with your trip, I knew you had plans." He shrugged, still smiling down at me. "It's your first time in England, I didn't want to disrupt anything. You always have me at home, but you only have England right now." His smile fell slightly as though just now realizing something. "Wait, why are you here?"

The question trailed off and I wasn't sure how to answer. I immediately felt as though I had let him down in some way. For so many years I had heard him talk about the United Kingdom as though it was a dream. A place far off that held part of his heart.

Why hadn't I made a better effort to get to know this place? This place he so dearly loved?

"Well, I-I was actually about to fly home, but this weather," I gestured behind me.

He narrowed his eyes slightly, as though trying to read through my words. His look made me fidget, the seriousness in his gaze always too perceptive. Why did I always get the feeling he understood me?

I shrugged and was relieved when those dark eyes of his lightened.

"It seems British hospitality has been lost on you. What a shame." He clicked his tongue, teasing.

"No, not lost. But maybe I'm so used to Southern hospitality I didn't recognize it." I offered.

"I doubt that," he said, tucking a hand into the pocket of his jeans. I suddenly realized I hardly ever saw him dressed like this. So casual and yet more formal than the sweaty t-shirts and work jeans he wore in the shop. Dressed in a cream-colored long sleeve shirt with buttons near the throat, dark jeans, and a black jacket covering his shoulders—the look was different, but somehow suited him.

"What are you going to do?" I asked, pulling my attention away from the broadness of his shoulders. How had I never noticed how large he was? He took up more space than I'd ever noticed before. I swallowed, wondering at this new reaction. "I'm guessing your connecting flight is canceled?"

He nodded. "Yeah, nothing going to Inverness. I'm renting a car and planning to see how far I can get before the weather sets in. I should be able to make it."

"How long of a drive?"

"Ten hours."

"Ten hours! You won't make it halfway."

He shrugged, "I'll just stop somewhere."

"Are there lots of places to stop?" I was suddenly concerned. What if he got stuck in the snow along some random highway or old road?

"Plenty," he smiled. "Why, are you worried?"

"Yes," I admitted.

"Good," he winked. And then glanced over his shoulder. "They told me it'll be a minute before my car is ready. Want to get something to eat while I wait? Unless you have to get going."

I shook my head. "My plans are shot, so yeah, let's do it." I then did a weird hop and some finger guns that I immediately regretted. Perhaps it was the mere fact that I felt lighthearted for the first time in over a week.

We found a nearby bar and ordered an appetizer and some sodas while we killed time. I suddenly didn't know what I was waiting for, but at least I could spend some time with Roland before we went our separate ways. All it took was him asking one question about my trip and everything came out.

I told him about Newbury and the disappointment of Highclere Castle. Not so much the castle, but the circumstances. In my voice, I could hear the longing to not feel so inept—the longing for experiences and to be taken by surprise by something. Perhaps it was that nagging sense of adventure in my gut.

I wondered if Roland could hear the yearning in my voice too.

"And this is Beardsley," I said, swiping through my phone to the picture of me with that horse. "He was rather pompous if you ask me."

Roland laughed. "Don't you know that is the only way they make horses in England?"

"He did remind me of a snobby butler," I grinned. "And we moved so slow, Roland you have no idea! Whatever happened to horses thundering across the countryside?"

"Do you even know how to do that?" he asked.

I grimaced. "It happened once."

"Really?" he questioned, doubting.

"Okay, so my dad took me riding and my horse bolted." Roland snorted at my words. "No, stop that," I laughed. "It wasn't my fault, it got spooked and just took off. I was twelve!"

He continued to laugh and I found myself grinning. "Sounds like you need a lesson."

I shrugged. "You know I've had years of lessons, and I know how to canter and even gallop." It was true, I did know how to handle a horse, but to just run across the countryside was something I'd never done before. Thinking of the expanse of days before me with this blizzard, I wondered if there was somewhere, I could go to fulfill that dream. But that didn't make any sense. I was no horse master, but if planes couldn't fly then horses probably didn't leave their barns.

"Well, if you ever get to Scotland, we'll go and, how did you say it, 'Thunder across the countryside'?"

"Only it will be the Scottish countryside," I countered and he nodded. "Just promise me that my horse will take some interest in the ride."

He laughed, his Adam's apple bobbing. "He didn't like you?"

"No! I mean look at him," I pointed to the picture on my phone again, "he was so disinterested in me, and for some odd reason, I liked him all the more for it."

My smile faltered slightly as I suddenly realized what I had said. Mason was certainly disinterested in me. Is that why I liked him? What a terrifying thought. But even as I pushed it away, I knew there was some truth to it. Some fear lingered there that I didn't want to explore.

Roland's phone buzzed on the table—he glanced at it before tucking it away. "So, you're already heading home? There's nothing else you want to do while you're here?"

"Well, I had thought about going to Chatsworth. It's the house they used for Pemberley—Mr. Darcy's home in *Pride and Prejudice*."

He nodded. "The 2005 version."

I stared at him. "You've seen it?"

He shrugged and when I laughed, he explained. "It's one of my mother's favorite movies. So yes, I have seen it." When I cackled again, he grinned sheepishly.

"I don't think so, I bet you're a secret fan, Roland Harmon." I couldn't contain my teasing. How had I never known this about him? "You have a secret romantic heart, don't you?" I laughed and he shook his head again, his lips quirking as he forced himself not to smile. "Admit it, I bet I could prove it."

"And how would you do that?" he was immediately curious. Turning the tables. How did he do that, meet my challenge, and immediately put me to the test?

"I'm not sure, but I bet I could figure out a way."

"Is that a challenge?"

"Maybe." I raised my chin, still teasing.

"And what if I could prove that you're a romantic too, Danielle Winthers?"

I rolled my eyes, "That's no real secret."

He pursed his lips. "What if I could prove something else?"

"And what is that something else?" I asked curiously. There was a gleam in his eyes that at once enticed me and made me feel as though I was standing at the edge of a cliff. I wanted to look closer but feared the fall. Confused, my smile faltered. He pursed his lips, judging something—hesitating.

His phone buzzed again, breaking the tension between us. This time he took a moment to type something and hit send. "Not the car yet," he sighed and ran a hand through his hair.

"Bummer," I said, knowing I didn't mean it.

This—talking with Roland—was the happiest I had felt in a long time. Friendship was such a treasure and the distance had only made me more aware of it. I wondered why it had never felt like this when he left to visit his grandparents. Sometimes he'd spent weeks away from Landing only to come back and tell me of his travels. Of course, during those days I had missed him, but nothing like this.

I suddenly felt like I had been needing him, needing his friendship.

"Why aren't you going to Chatsworth?" he asked suddenly, not resuming our earlier challenge. I was slightly gratified he didn't.

"It's closed to visitors right now."

His brow furrowed, "Really? That seems odd. I know it isn't peak season, but..." he trailed off.

"But...?" I prompted.

He came back around, "They should still be open."

"Their website says they're closed."

"Hmmm," was the only sound he made. He looked toward one of the windows and then abruptly stood. "I'll be right back."

I saw him put his phone to his ear and waited for him to return. Our waiter took away the empty plate of fries, or chips, as they were called. I waited, my foot tapping, and checked my phone.

Roland came back around the corner and slid into his chair. "So, about that bet..." he quirked an eyebrow. I laughed.

"Yes?"

"My grandmother knows a curator and some of the tour guides at Chatsworth, they'll let us in if you want to go."

"Really?" my eyes widened. I had forgotten Roland's grandparents had spent most of their careers as historians, professors, and curators. They had connections all over the world. I'd often figured they'd decided to retire in Scotland just for the sheer amount of history surrounding them.

"Yes," he grinned, but there was a wicked, teasing gleam in his eyes. "But you have to promise you'll be honest with me if we make this bet."

"Okay, but what do you have to prove? You still haven't told me that part."

He peered at me for a moment as though debating something. For some odd reason, I had the feeling he was uncertain, I could see it in his eyes before it cleared and he took a deep breath Whatever had given him pause was now a challenge he would meet head-on.

For reasons I couldn't explain, my stomach tightened in anticipation. Our game had suddenly grown serious; real emotions at stake.

When he next spoke, it was almost a husky whisper. "You can try and prove that I'm a romantic," his gaze remained transfixed on me, "but I will prove that your heart belongs here."

My brow furrowed; it was an odd thing to say. "What here in England?"

He shrugged, the expression casual, but when I looked into his eyes, they were anything but unconcerned. In his dark gaze, I saw the burning of some sort of emotion I couldn't name.

I swallowed as the silence between us grew.

Well, if he wasn't going to answer then I would set the terms.

"All right, I will prove you're a romantic, or at least you're a sap for romantic movies," I tacked that on and watched him roll his eyes, "and you're going to prove that my heart belongs in England."

"That it belongs here," he clarified.

"Right," I said and extended my hand. "Challenge accepted on my part. Are you a betting man?" I smiled, enjoying this new game.

Roland looked at my hand and held up a finger. "On one condition."

"What's that?"

"That we're honest with each other."

I swallowed. He knew me better than most. I was always honest, except in matters of the heart. Except in those things that pulled at what I kept hidden from the world. Inhaling deeply, I stuck my hand out more firmly. I could do this—I could take this leap.

"Deal," I said.

"Deal." Roland grasped my hand and shook it.

I smiled and realized a new kind of adventure was about to begin. May the skies be blessed for having canceled our individual plans.

"Now come on," Roland said, throwing his backpack over his shoulder and some money on the table. "The car is ready and we have a three-hour drive to Chatsworth."

"Wait, what about your grandparents?"

"Nan just told me she doesn't want me on the roads either. And since Chatsworth is only three hours away, we can make it before this blizzard hits."

"Barely," I said softly, debating. Reason won out. We had already shaken on it, and I wasn't the sort of friend to go back on my word. Who was I to complain? I was headed to Chatsworth. Perhaps Mr. Darcy was there after all.

Laughing at that thought, I threw my backpack over my shoulder and followed Roland out of the restaurant. We stepped into sleet and flung our things into the awaiting car. As I slid into the passenger seat, Roland winked at me from behind the wheel.

"Ready?" he asked.

"Ready!" I said with some excitement I couldn't contain. A new adventure awaited, and this time my friend was going with me. For the first time since leaving Landing, I was truly excited.

And with a bet on the line, I knew I would win if it was the last thing I did. If I couldn't prove he was a romantic, I would do everything within my power to keep my heart tucked safely away.

I'd been doing it for years; how hard could it truly be?

CHAPTER 10

Dark clouds rolled across the countryside, following our car. Though sleet and rain had kept the wipers busy for the last three hours, we were finally slowing as we reached Bakewell, a quaint town not far from Chatsworth House. Roland had guessed it was the best place to spend the night.

Not long after leaving the airport, I found I enjoyed riding in the car as opposed to driving. Perhaps because I wasn't having to worry about going the wrong way on a roundabout.

We'd spent most of the trip talking, though about what I couldn't remember. It seemed that every word I'd held back in the past week of solo travel, was now pouring from my mouth. Often when I glanced over at Roland, he was smiling with one hand on the wheel as he listened. Something about this place suited him— relaxed him. It reminded me of how he was in his workshop. His hands steady, his mind focused and yet at ease. Only in his workshop was he completely at peace with the world, but perhaps England was another contender for his affection.

The hotel booked our room for the night and sent us along a yellow hallway and up a thin staircase. I had the distinct feeling we were getting the cheap rooms as the rest of the hallways were lined with red carpet.

Roland tripped on the rug as we entered our room and I teased him before throwing my bag on one of the twin beds. Flopping back, the springs squeaked in protest.

"I shouldn't be tired, but I am," I sighed.

"Me too," Roland yawned and I heard him opening up his bag. "Should we grab dinner?"

"Probably," I agreed. It felt like a whole day had passed since leaving London. What were we going to do for the rest of the day?

"I think we got quite the discount."

I leaned up on my elbows and laughed to find Roland looking around the room, his hands in the pockets of his jeans. The room was sparse, two of the pictures on the walls were crooked, and I was a little afraid to look in the bathroom. There was no way Roland's broad shoulders were going to be able to fit through that door without him turning sideways. Sure enough, he peeked inside and had to twist to fit.

"Come look at this shower!" he said, turning back to me, his eyes gleaming.

"What?" I rose and padded across the floor. Looking inside, I began to laugh. I would be lucky to fit inside the glass door, but the showerhead couldn't have been higher than my forehead. I looked at Roland, who was 6'4, up and down. "Have fun with that."

He laughed. And moved away from me toward the wall. Maybe it was the drive or the release of stress, but when he tried to straighten the picture and it went right back, I snorted with a laugh. He tried again and it did the same thing.

"It will just have to do," he chuckled and together we both let the stress from the day fall away as our shoulders shook. Over and over again, I continued to break out in laughter, for some reason that stupid picture swinging on the hook was too much. Coupled with the image of Roland attempting to shower and I couldn't pull myself together.

After a while, we both steadied, gathering our breaths as though our lungs were starved for attention. The bed squeaked beneath my back as I rolled over to look at where Roland sat in a chair by the window.

A question that had been forming in my mind all day took precedence. "So, about this bet... how are you going to prove me wrong?"

"Why would I reveal my secrets?" he asked.

I shrugged, "You're the one who said that we have to be honest."

"That doesn't mean I can't just stay silent."

"Dually noted," I saluted him.

"Wait, wait," he back-tracked, realizing that I'd caught him, his cheeks still flushed from laughter. I had always liked the way the lines around his mouth stayed creased. "That's not how this works."

"How should it work?"

He pursed his lips and thought for a moment. "How about when I ask a question, and if you answer it, you get to ask me one? And vice versa."

It seemed reasonable enough, so why did I feel as though there was a risk to this game? As much as I didn't want to answer his questions truthfully, there were parts of me that wanted him to tell me his secrets. Flashes of that night from so many years ago came to mind. That tear he'd shed on the trampoline was as much a mystery to me today as it had been that night. We'd never spoken of it, and to remember how he'd looked … I wondered if I could ever dare to ask him.

Our friendship had developed over the years. Going from acquaintances in a group to confidants when it came to our struggles, our families, our hopes and dreams. But somewhere along the way, our paths had forked. Of course, we still conversed, we spent time in friendly conversation and studying one another, but did I truly know who Roland was? There was such a great difference between being friends and intimately knowing the workings of a person's heart. I could easily predict what Roland was doing most times of the day, I could pick out what he would eat at a restaurant, I knew the names of his childhood dogs, his favorite places in the world, but there were lots of things about him that were unknown to me.

So many things. Who he truly was in his heart was often a mystery.

The daunting realization of the bet I had made grew.

"Shall I get us started?" he asked, quirking an eyebrow.

My gut tightened. I wasn't ready for this. The enormity of what I had agreed to settled. What had I done?

He focused his gaze solely upon me, all mirth had retreated from his lips. I paused, waiting, even as my heart thrummed.

"Dani?"

"Yes?" I asked, my voice came out a little higher than I would have liked.

He held my eyes for a moment, all seriousness. Nerves gripped my stomach. "What would you like to eat for dinner?"

I blinked, then grimaced as a smile broke out over his lips. I threw a pillow at him. He laughed. "You're the worst!"

He tossed the pillow onto my bed. "Answer the question."

"Anything," I said.

"And that's the truth?"

"Let me change that," I held up a finger, "I meant anything that I like. With the way you are right now, you'll probably have me eating blood pudding."

He grinned as though that was exactly what he had been thinking.

I stood, placing my hands on my hips. "My turn."

His smile grew wider and when he nodded, he rose from the chair by the window and moved closer to me. My full intention had been to taunt him as much as he had me. I had planned to bait and draw him in, but I was lost for words as he moved closer. Tilting my chin back, I met his gaze as he stared down at me.

Perhaps this small hotel room made him seem taller than usual, and there were the single beds to be thought of too. Everything here was petite, quaint, and in essence, it made him all the broader, larger—more masculine. I was used to seeing him in his workshop and outside, but here, well my breath was certainly caught in my throat for a moment.

I blinked, uncertain of what I was feeling. Nothing like this had ever happened before.

Roland lowered his chin to look at me more fully, this time the humor in his eyes had disappeared. Something pinched my gut and I worked to clear my thoughts. He thought he was the only one who could play games? He had another thing coming.

"You were going to ask me something?"

I nodded but didn't say a word. Leaning back slightly, I bit my lip and watched as his eyes dipped to my mouth. "I was wondering when you became such a ridiculous flirt. It was well played, but," I tossed my hair over my shoulder, "you'll have to do better than that."

I winked, a wicked grin sliding across my lips.

That caught him, surprise brightening his eyes. He'd never seen me like this.

A little triumphant, I walked to the door knowing that I had at least succeeded in setting him as off-kilter as he had me. If this was to be a game, I would try and win.

"Well done," he murmured behind me as we left the room.

I wasn't entirely certain why those two words sent a shiver along my spine.

CHAPTER 11

Some lines of friendship should never be crossed. Boundaries, nearly invisible, but set up for the sake of simple normalcy.

Perhaps my childhood was different than some, but the rules in my house while growing up were finite. I was not allowed to sleep in the same room as a boy. As a family, I'd slept in hotel rooms with my brother, him usually on the floor, and my sister and me in the bed. One night, Henry had kept me and Anna awake late into the night with his snoring and I remember telling her I might kill him. We had laughed, and somewhere in the darkness of early morning, we'd fallen asleep.

But right now, there was no one to laugh with and this newness with Roland was the slightest bit unsettling.

I was laying in the darkened room, listening to a sound I had never heard before. In all our years of friendship, I'd never seen Roland asleep. I'd never heard the slumbering breaths he now took—their relaxing depth lulling me into a state of relaxation, and at the same time putting me on edge.

How could he fall asleep so easily?

Biting my lip, I glanced at the opposing twin bed. My heart was thundering in my chest. We'd crossed a line—some line that marked an intimate boundary.

Our friendship had always been so simple, so easy to explain. I could have wrapped it up in a perfect little box with a bow on top. The lid would have fit perfectly and inside was the explanation of what we were. *Friends.*

But now… I didn't know what to think. Perhaps it was being in England, or something in the air, but things had changed. That lid no longer fit so easily, and what was inside, I dared not look.

It was our bet, and this—this change in seeing him differently. It was assaulting my senses and shifting my focus. I didn't know what to think.

Inhaling deeply, I rolled onto my side and watched as Roland's shoulder rose and fell with each breath. I had never wondered what he looked like while he slept—had never thought about how he seemed to favor sleeping on his right, my favorite side too. Why that mattered I didn't know.

Frustrated, I rolled to my left so as not to look at him anymore. There in the darkness of the room, I closed my eyes and tried to drift off to sleep.

I would have thought I'd be tired after such a long day, but the rest of my body wouldn't cooperate. Everything from family to Mason shifted through my mind. I wondered what Mason was doing and if Nancy was in Landing yet—she probably was and Mason was showing her all the best places in town. Rolling onto my back, I stared up at the ceiling.

It still hurt. I hated to admit it, but rejection had a sting that lingered in deep places.

A tear rolled from my eye and into my hair. It didn't matter that Mason was happy, it didn't matter that it wasn't his fault, it still hurt. To be overlooked and cast aside seemed to always be my lot.

I wondered if the rejection would have hurt more if I'd had the chance to ask, or if it would sting just the same. His dismissal wasn't outright, but simply that he didn't see me as someone he wanted to date, and he didn't consider me worth noticing. I'd been there at the wedding when he'd seen Nancy—when he'd danced with her. Did he know I wished for him to look at me that way?

Fiddling with the blankets that were pulled across my chest, I wondered about my faithful, fictional companion. She was a companion of thought—a sort of muse to understand my situation. More than anything, Charlotte Lucas was a trapped woman, a woman who was forced to be practical. She didn't have the luxury of a fairytale like Elizabeth. She hadn't caught the eye of the hero. Instead, she chose to save herself and marry Mr. Collins.

Another tear escaped. Was something like that to be my fate?

Roland had told me to take a leap of faith, but it felt more like I was running away. Was that what Charlotte had done? Had she run away in fear of her future?

Though she was just a character, I felt such companionship with her. My fear was ever-present, weighing upon me. Perhaps Roland was right, someday I would have to take a leap of faith. But what if you didn't know which cliff you were meant to jump from?

Glancing toward Roland, I wondered what he would say to that. Deep down, I knew I would never tell him. For I had never told anyone how afraid I truly was.

To allow someone to see those depths of my soul could potentially shatter me. It would awaken a longing in me that if released and denied would break me completely. No, it was better to stay safe, to not leap.

After some time, I realized I was still watching Roland. Transfixed, my eyes remained on him with each deep breath that expanded his shoulders slightly before releasing. Closing my eyes, the lull of his breaths drew me closer and closer to sleep, until like a drifting wind, all thought left and I slipped into unconsciousness.

CHAPTER 12

Everything looked different in the light of morning. The winter fields were patched with ice and snow, the hills rolling over one another in gentle slopes as we passed along the winding road toward Chatsworth House. The expansive estate spread much further than I could see and as we rounded a curve I gasped. There, was the house.

I didn't care that its real name was Chatsworth. To me, it was Pemberley.

The stone walls on either side of the road broke away as we descended a hill, the side of the stately home to our right. I couldn't look away.

"Oh my," I whispered, placing a hand to my mouth. "It's so beautiful."

Roland laughed and out of the corner of my eye, I saw him glance my way. As though perfectly timed, a herd of deer ran across a sloping hill and near the car before veering toward the trees like a flock of birds. I shook my head. It was like a dream.

When we pulled up to the gate, Roland said something to the guard on duty, but I hardly noticed. I was too busy gawking at the looming house that took up my entire line of sight. It was so incredible, powerful, breathtaking. As we came to a stop, I hurried out of the car and stared in wonder—curiosity sparking and tingling my senses. There was something in the air of places with history; unknown secrets dangling, their mysteries so tantalizing to the mind.

"I guess even your imagination couldn't top this?" Roland asked.

I shook my head. "I'm at a loss for words. I just, I mean, look at it!"

Roland chuckled. "Come on, Nan said Alexander would meet us at the entrance."

Hardly looking where I was going, I followed Roland, unable to keep my eyes off of the place that held a piece of my imaginative heart. *Oh, Pemberley.*

How was I ever going to put the right words together to correctly describe this sense of wonder for Mrs. Kent? Here, the very air was fresh and alive with new possibilities.

As we reached the entrance, an excitable man called out to us from behind a ticket counter.

"Morning!" His face split into a cheerful grin, his cheeks rosy as though chapped. He had a gap between his front teeth, eyes that squinted when he smiled, and one of those faces that was so expressive it could change on a mere whim. I had the distinct notion that even my father, who was deaf, would be able to understand this man without any assistance.

"Alexander?" Roland asked.

"Yes, yes," Alexander confirmed, rising from his chair and coming around the corner. His hands were braced on two walking crutches and though he walked with a slight tilt in his hips, he moved rather quickly. Placing one crutch over his forearm he stuck out his hand to me, and then Roland.

"You must be Louise and Elton's grandson. How do you do?" His eyebrows wiggled. "My name is," and he tilted back as though speaking to the heavens with a definitive air, "Alexander Baron Michael James Holton." He winked at me. "Terribly pretentious, isn't it?"

I laughed.

"You may simply call me Alexander. Now, shall we begin our tour? As you know we are closed to all tourists today, but anything for Louise and Elton. Is there something you wish to see first?"

I bit my lip, his accent and manner were so inviting. Nearly bouncing on my heels, I glanced at Roland. "I-I hadn't thought about it. I would love to see everything."

"Everything? Ha!" Alexander tilted backward again, his spine curving as he spoke to the air. He had the oddest mannerisms and I liked him all the more for them. "We have over three hundred rooms, seventeen staircases, and three hundred and fifty doors, and she says she wants to see everything!" He chuckled. "Oh, you will see plenty, and we will begin presently. Now, make like the Red Sea and part."

I stared at him in confusion until he cackled, raised both of his canes, and motioned for us to separate. Roland caught on faster and stepped aside, his grin growing wider.

Alexander walked between us, calling over his shoulder, "You have no idea how many times I've used that line on tours and people stare at me like I'm an idiot." He chuckled, his cheer warming his cheeks. "But I would rather be an idiot than a grump, wouldn't you say?"

"I can agree with that," Roland laughed. He held his hand out to me and I took it, smiling up at him. This place was as magical as I had wanted it to be. For all the disappointment of Highclere Castle, here was the adventure I'd been longing for.

I didn't speak as Alexander led us through a hall and into the house, his canes tapping on the floors. His voice boomed in the empty rooms as we moved from one part of the house to the other. In places like this, I was always tempted to whisper, as though not to disturb the greatness of history that lingered in the shadows. But not Alexander. No, his voice filled the rooms and echoed along the hallways. He was at home in this place, and it made Pemberley all the more fascinating.

As the tour stretched on, my neck grew tired from constantly craning upward to take in the intricate ceilings painted by Italian artists. Every now and then I snapped pictures when allowed, but not as often as I expected. As much as this place was beautiful, it was posh, grand, royal, but not comfortable or homey.

Just then, we rounded a corner and a sight I knew well opened before us. The sun was breaking through the clouds, and out upon the reflecting pond, a fountain shot high into the air. Alexander went on about the power of the fountain and the importance of its place on the estate. Roland asked him some questions about the mechanics of it all, but I tuned everything out as I watched a spark of sunlight shimmer through the water—a rainbow lighting the window for the blink of a moment.

Everything about this place was dripping wealth and power, and yet it was inviting, not in a lecherous way, but a magical way—almost fairytale-like.

"Come on," Roland whispered. The first words he'd spoken to me in a long time. Alexander was nearly out of the room and I hadn't even noticed as I'd been too engrossed by the view.

"Do you think we'll get a chance to go outside?"

"We can ask."

I nodded, wrapping my other hand around Roland's while trying not to think about how I liked holding his in mine. His fingers squeezed, applying gentle pressure before pulling me along.

Alexander led us upstairs and it was here that his voice lowered, but secrets must often be told with a little mischievousness. "Have you ever heard of Georgianna Cavendish the Duchess of Devonshire?" He asked, his eyes gleaming. "Now, come with me, it is time I tell the tales that have long been whispered through these halls."

I smiled and followed him, clinging to his every word as he brought the ages of the past to life all around us. There was a moment as he was talking that I told myself to pay attention because I wanted so desperately to remember this place—to remember every detail. Like a performer on the grandest stage, he weaved tales, rumors, and myths, bringing the past to life as though the ghosts of the house were drifting through the very walls.

"Were you here when they filmed *Pride and Prejudice*?" I asked as we descended a staircase a few hours later.

Alexander barked, "Ha! I spotted you as a Jane Austen fan."

"What gave me away?"

"Well, you're a woman in England." He chuckled, concentrating on his canes as they clipped along the stairs. "You ladies love a little Austen, but do you want to know a secret?"

"Another one?" I smiled, enjoying his banter.

"I love her too."

I laughed. "So, you were here then?"

"Ah, no. I was away at hospital." He gestured toward his legs. "But, I wish I had been. I've heard it was quite an exciting time."

I tucked a strand of hair behind my ear. "I'm sure it was. This place is just…" I couldn't find the right words.

"I know," an undercurrent of seriousness and companionship laced his voice. "I've toured this house more times than I can count and yet, I always see something new. She's a beauty, rare indeed, and with so many layers."

It was only when we were halfway across the hall that I realized Roland hadn't followed us. I turned to find him staring at a painting of a woman. "Is this her?" he asked, pointing.

Alexander beamed, "You've found her! I was wondering who would spot her first. Another game of mine," he chuckled, please with himself.

"Who? Georgianna?"

"The very one," Alexander nodded, his crutches silenced on the plush red carpet of the hall. "Isn't she beautiful? Makes me wonder what she would have been like to talk to."

We all stared at the painting, musing in silence. The Duchess wore an enormous hat, tipped slightly on her head. She was fashionable, her skin a creamy complexion—quite beautiful and certainly eye-catching. I wondered why I hadn't noticed the painting before, and felt guilty for not having spotted it.

Thinking of all Alexander had told us about this woman, I gazed at the portrait. She was as much a mystery as this house and the history that lived in these halls.

"She seems sad." Roland sighed beside me.

He was staring at the painting, his eyes gentle, and the creases around the edges of his mouth turned down at the corners. Looking back at the painting, I traced my eyes along the lines and found myself staring at the Duchess's face. Roland was right. It was in her face that the grandeur fell away. The artist, Gainsborough, had painted a depth to the eyes of this woman. It was there that the Duchess fell away to reveal the woman behind the façade. *Georgianna.*

"I think she was," Alexander whispered. "She was praised, famous throughout all of England, but I think she was very lonely and lost."

I couldn't tear my gaze away from her eyes. How had Roland spotted the longing in those eyes so quickly? The desperation and struggle to appear regal and yet seem lacking? Pursing my lips, I glanced back at Roland again, my heart thundering. I'd always known he was perceptive, but this was more than I realized.

Perhaps it was his eye for detail in his work. Whatever it was, I knew he saw more than he let on, and if that was true he knew me in more ways than I wished. Clearing my throat, I turned away from the painting and walked along the hall. Other images captured my mind, but the memory of Roland staring deep into Georgianna's eyes was one I wouldn't forget soon.

Our tour came to an end as Alexander led us outside onto the porch that overlooked the reflecting pool. Like inside, the sight took my breath away. Resting my hands along the stone, I gazed across the water as Roland came up beside me.

"So beautiful isn't it?" he asked.

I could only nod—words lost. "Maybe you are right," I teased, "perhaps my heart does belong here after all."

"I know it does," he said, his voice dipping low.

I gazed up at him then, only to find him smiling to himself. I laughed, breathlessly. "You haven't won yet," I grinned.

"But I'm getting closer," he winked.

Perhaps he was. This place was certainly as magical as I had hoped—that sense of adventure lingering. Maybe it was where my heart belonged.

"Let's have a picture," Alexander said from behind us, startling me. I had forgotten he was there. For just a moment it had been me and Roland—just like always.

I turned and Roland slung his arm around my shoulders as I wrapped my arm around his waist. When he poked me in the side I laughed and shook my head, only for Alexander to make some lewd comment that left us both grinning with red cheeks. I was certain I would have to delete those photos. All the same, Alexander Airdropped the pictures to our phones, before promising to meet us at the same time and place tomorrow morning for another tour.

The clicking of his crutches retreated and we set out along the reflecting pool, silence hanging between us. I was reminded of last night and the intimacy of darkness. Something was changing between us and I didn't know what to hold onto—my heart pounded.

I was bothered, and I didn't know what it was. Only when we were near the end of the pool and gazing back at the house did I realize what it was. Roland had been looking at Georgianna's painting as though he understood her. Not that he could see her sadness, but that he understood it.

The memory of his gaze that night in Landing when I left flashed in my memory, followed by the remembrance of a warm summer's evening and a trampoline. Was it possible that Roland was sad? That he was lonely?

Too many memories of his laughter and joyful hope flooded my mind. Could it even be possible?

Glancing at him now, I wondered what sort of bargain I had gotten myself into. I had planned to prove Roland was a romantic at heart, and I certainly knew he was now, but when I had made that bet, I thought it would mean he was a silly romantic—the kind that flooded chick-flicks and romantic novels. Nothing like this.

The wind tugged at my hair as we watched lights begin to decorate the windows of Chatsworth and reflect off the waters. The house itself seemed like it was floating—I felt like I was floating and drowning at the same time as the surety of what I'd seen in Roland's eyes solidified. Roland had understood the longing in that painting of Georgianna—a longing for something that when denied resided in sadness. I knew because I understood it too.

The only question was—what was Roland longing for?

Suddenly, I wondered if I even knew him. And more certain than ever before, I knew I was afraid to know the answer.

CHAPTER 13

"Now, there's a sight," Roland said, nodding toward the grand house, all the lights gleaming and winking at us as the sky darkened. Though it had been a week, it still surprised me how early the sun set with England being so far to the North.

"It is beautiful," I said, snapping a few pictures. "I think this is more what Mrs. Kent was going for."

"A bit grand, don't you think?"

"No, not that, this feeling," I corrected. When Roland didn't answer I continued. "A sort of magical, peace, or something like that. I'm not explaining it well."

"No, you aren't," he chuckled. "It's a good thing your job doesn't depend on words."

I gave a very unladylike snort. "Remind me again how you're able to build furniture while traveling the world?"

"The explanation you're looking for is *vacation*. Besides, I don't have the pressures you do, being so world-renowned and all."

"Oh yes," rolled my eyes, "my pressures are so many."

He smiled. "So, what do you like the most about this view?"

I squinted in concentration. "It's inviting. Like a warm hug after a long trip. It's that light at the end of the tunnel kind of feeling."

He nodded, "That sounds like Mrs. Kent."

"It does," I whispered, my thoughts taking me slowly elsewhere. Perhaps it wasn't the grand places she wanted to recreate at her Bed & Breakfast, but rather this feeling—this sense of fantastical amusement grounded in the comfort of being home. It was an interesting notion and one I wanted to explore further.

Walking away from Roland, I snapped a few more pictures of the water, this time focusing on the illuminated windows more than the house. Perhaps England was what Mrs. Kent wanted me to explore, not the places. Maybe it was this essence that seemed to be in the very air of Britain, this mysterious beckoning from a land that had stood the test of time. Rolling hills that had been ridden over by the Dukes of Devonshire and other powerful men and women throughout the years. Standing where I was now, I wondered if Georgianna had ever enjoyed this view. Alexander had told us when the grand reflecting pool was built, I simply didn't remember when.

I turned to ask Roland about it, only to realize he had walked a short distance away. There he stood along the side of the water, gazing at the house, his hands tucked into the pockets of his jacket, his back to me, and the dark waves of his hair lifting gently in the sharp winter breeze. Bending slightly, I hurried to snap a picture of him before he moved—the windows of Chatsworth gleaming behind him as he stood resolute. It reminded me so much of the way he'd stood looking at Georgianna's painting. A deep longing beckoning from within. Biting my lip, I watched, wondering where his mind was.

"Are you hungry?" He asked. I jumped and tucked my phone away.

"Since we skipped lunch?" I nodded. "I could eat."

"Good," he nodded, "me too. Shall we?" He beckoned with his head and I nodded, following him. A sharp wind tugged at our coats and tickled my nose. When I sneezed, I apologized and Roland laughed.

"You know being here, it makes me feel like I should be the one apologizing. I should have a handkerchief or something of that sort."

"Who carries a handkerchief nowadays anyways?"

"I don't know, but it seems like a very British thing to do."

"But your family is Scottish, right?"

A small smile curved his lips, "Yes, but so far back I don't remember how many generations it goes. I'm probably more other things than Scottish."

"Ahh," I agreed, "we're all a mix of one thing or another."

"True," he nodded, pursing his lips. "But that still doesn't give me an excuse for being improper. I mean, would Mr. Collins have been caught without a handkerchief?"

"Mr. Collins? Why would you pick him as the proper one?"

"Well, if he is the most ridiculous and still carried a handkerchief, then I must really be lacking."

For some reason, the idea of Roland comparing himself to Mr. Collins offended me. He was anything but cowering and belittling to others, and he certainly wasn't foolish. Mr. Collins was a character I refused to associate with my best friend.

"You're nothing like Mr. Collins," I said. That earned me a side-long glance from across the hood of the car as he unlocked it.

"I'm not?" he asked, leaning his arm on the hood.

I shook my head. "No, not at all."

"So, you think I'm all British and proper?" His eyes gleamed, teasing.

"I didn't say that," I rolled my eyes. "I said you're not like him, but I don't know if Jane Austen would approve of you." There let him deal with that.

He pretended to look insulted as we swung into the car. "Give me one reason Jane Austen wouldn't like me."

I laughed, enjoying our game. "Well for starters, you don't come with a title or money."

"Ahh, that's a shame."

"Isn't it? And on top of that, you work with your hands. Regency ladies would have thought you a farmer."

He placed a hand to his forehead. "Why did I choose to be a carpenter? I will be alone forever."

"It's a shame." I sighed. "And then, there is the matter of our friendship," I said, laughing. Roland stilled beside me as though waiting. "If we were living in Jane Austen's time my reputation would be in tatters—ruins. I spent last night at a local inn with a man I'm not married to, and no chaperone in sight."

Roland barked out a laugh. "What would Austen do with you?"

"Probably cast me as Lydia."

He chuckled and started the car. "Does that make me Wickham?"

I sighed. "Roland, you don't see yourself the way others do." He glanced at me, and then we pulled out of the parking lot.

I silently cursed myself, wondering how quickly I had let the game between us drop and the raw emotion to fall between us. Did I think Roland didn't see himself clearly? Yes. But to tell him was a different kind of conversation than I was willing to have. It seemed England was unraveling the careful rules I had constructed over the years.

Just then my stomach grumbled and I pressed a hand to my stomach. "To answer your question, yes, I'm hungry."

Roland just smiled, one hand on the steering wheel, the other on the gear shift as we rolled over the hills and back toward Bakewell.

After a dinner of roast duck, served with mashed taters and vegetables, was picked clean from my plate, I settled back in my chair with a glass of wine in reach. We had found a quaint little restaurant near one of the roundabouts in Bakewell, not far from the inn where we were staying. It was a charming place, all warm and cozy with deep mahogany walls, plush, curve-backed chairs, and heavy curtains parted along the windows. The gleam of a few lampposts lining the street was blurred in the waved glass.

Snowflakes fell lazily, as though without commitment, the white specks swaying in the wind.

Sinking deeper into my chair, I rested my hand along the stem of my wine glass, my comfortable sweater and leggings helping to contribute to this feeling of lethargy that was spreading through me.

When the waitress asked me if I would like another glass, I nodded and thanked her after she poured the white wine and turned to leave. Roland was staring out the window too, both of us content as the fire in the hearth behind my back warmed the room.

My thoughts drifted, wondering what my family was doing. I had emailed my parents to let them know I would be in England longer than I'd originally planned.

Anna had been asking for details and had shared in my astonishment the chances of running into Roland. She was now convinced that I was never coming back to Landing. I'd laughed at that—I knew I would return, even if the idea was appealing. I would simply enjoy my time here while I could.

If there was one thing I had learned in my twenty-seven years it was the way life had a means of changing on a whim. You could go years without a change, a monotonous slew of daily tasks, and then with a snap, everything could be altered.

That's what this trip felt like. A shift—a change of the winds.

What that change was, I didn't know, and quite frankly, was afraid to find out.

Glancing at the time on the mantle I counted backward and figured my dad was probably taking his lunch break—he worked remotely as a video game designer of all things. As an artist, he had the unique ability and drive to see the world differently. Perhaps it was the fact that he was deaf. He navigated the world in an altered manner, but his patience and persistence always inspired me.

And his ability to listen.

Though deaf, he was the best listener I knew. When someone talks to him, he gives his full attention—reading lips, nodding along, and understanding on a much deeper level than most. When I was little, I remembered learning sign language and how other kids thought it was weird, but they didn't know the benefits. I'd had secret conversations in church with my dad while no one was the wiser. Sometimes he'd make me laugh on purpose.

Thinking of it now, I smiled. One time, Mason had asked what I was doing. His family usually sat across the aisle from mine and he'd noticed my hands twitching in my lap. That was when I was old enough to sign the sermon to my dad. My mom used to do it, but every now and then she let me as I got older.

That was the day my crush on Mason had started. A young girl being noticed by the charming boy at church. It had grown from then on—parts of me were still ashamed to admit that my heart longed for him. I, a grown woman of twenty-seven, was still in love with a boy from her childhood.

Jane Austen wouldn't know what to do with me. Or maybe she would, often her heroines were deep thinkers and passionate, secret lovers of souls.

"I think we're doing a rather terrible job with our bet," Roland mused.

"Hmm?" I asked, his words hardly registering. I replayed them and blinked, coming back to the present. "How so?"

Memories of childhood and teenage-crushed hearts dissipated. Simpler times, simply fled.

"I should be asking you more questions to win."

"One problem though," I held up a finger as Roland turned to face me, the creases along the sides of his mouth arcing slightly, "we never said what we would win. What's a bet without a prize?"

His eyes drifted down to his fingers, where he picked at the table cloth. "We can worry about that part later."

I shrugged in response, even though he didn't see it. "Still seems pointless to bet when there's nothing to win."

"Not even for the pure knowledge of just being right?"

How could I tell him I already knew he was a romantic at heart? My bet had been less than risky, so why had I agreed to it?

Perhaps because of the earnest look he had given me in the airport. He'd wanted the challenge and needed me to agree. But why I didn't understand.

"Well, if we were serious gamblers, what kind of questions would you ask me?"

He seemed to ponder that for a moment. "I might ask you why you came back to Landing after college."

I took a sip of wine to mask the sharp prick of that question. "Are you asking that now?"

His eyes met mine, a lingering seriousness slightly hidden there. My heart began to pound heavily in my chest.

The lines that slightly crinkled at the edges of his eyes captured my attention. How had I never noticed them before? Probably because I had always focused on his nose. I liked his nose—always had. It was large, hooked, but gave his face prominence and character.

I shook those thoughts away. They were two-glasses-of-wine thoughts, the kinds of thoughts that made it through my normal barriers of defense.

His fingers played with the table cloth, smoothing it over and over again, but his gaze remained on my face for a few seconds. "I am asking." His voice dipped lower, intimate.

I shrugged in my warm sweater and took another sip. "I realized I didn't like being so far from home."

"We promised to tell the truth," he countered, and then offered, "and you'll get to ask me something next."

I pursed my lips, seeing the dangling reward. I thought of that night on the trampoline, would he tell me what had upset him? It was a gamble, but was I willing to risk it? As an unspoken rule, Roland and I didn't talk about these sorts of things. But everything else had been upended here, why not these deep feelings too?

Taking a deep breath for courage, I forged over the wall that we'd carefully constructed between us through the years. I could do this, I would do this.

"I—I wasn't sure about what to do with my life." I shrugged, hating the way my voice came out all shaky. "I was scared because nothing had turned out the way I thought it would."

His brow furrowed. "You mean getting married."

I nodded and pushed back against the tears threatening there. It was a raw, familiar wound, and one that I struggled to keep from festering.

"I just wanted that part of my life to begin, and I didn't view it like a child. At least not then. Of course, when I was little I thought Prince Charming would come and sweep me off my feet, but life shows you that's not true. And that's not what I was looking for, or even am looking for now. I just," I took a deep, shaky breath, "I just get so frustrated sometimes, you know. It's not like most things in life where you can set goals and then go do it. But this, I don't know how to make it happen and somewhere along the way I missed the boat—and now I don't know what to do."

Tears escaped and I suddenly realized my hold on my emotions was slipping. I wiped away the tears with my sleeve. "I'm sorry."

"Don't apologize," Roland murmured, still watching me too closely. I couldn't even look at him directly—too afraid of what I would see there.

I curled one leg up onto my chair and wrapped my arms around it. "It's just, I hate feeling like this. Like, I don't understand what I did wrong. All my life I was raised to focus on school, to be smart, to get good grades and not worry about boys, and to set myself up for a career. We live in this society of 'you can have it all,' and then there was this flip that happened midway through college. Suddenly everyone expected me to be dating, to be on my way to marriage, and I wasn't. And ever since then, I've had to pretend. I've had to walk around acting like I'm this strong, independent woman, and I am, but inside I am longing to simply be loved. And it just hurts to be rejected so many times." I sniffed, hating how snot always threatened to run down my face when I cried. "And it's not that I'm bad, or that the men I was interested in were wrong, it just hasn't fit and I don't know if it ever will."

Roland remained silent for a long time, letting me compose myself. He handed me one of the cloth napkins.

"Now you have a handkerchief," I said, coughing out a laugh.

One side of his mouth lifted, but it didn't reach his eyes. He opened his mouth to speak and then closed it.

"Don't feel like you have to say anything. It's just a lot of what I've been thinking, and to answer your question fully," I ran a hand in my hair and flipped it, "I moved back to Landing because some part of me gave up. I gave up trying to fit my life into the mold I had always dreamed of."

"And you've done well for yourself," Roland said, his voice quieter than I had ever heard it.

"I have," I nodded.

"But it's not what you've wanted most, is it?"

I shook my head, unable to speak for a moment as another bout of tears pooled. "So many women want these big careers, and I have nothing against that, it's just not what I want. I've so wanted to be like my mom, to start a family and raise kids, and that just doesn't seem possible now."

"You're only twenty-seven, Dani. I think you need to take a step back and look at the big picture."

I nodded. Not entirely certain if I agreed. "I mean you're single," I waved a hand toward him. "Do you ever feel like you missed some memo?"

He shrugged, "Sometimes, but in a different way."

"How so?" I asked, curious.

"Is this your question for today?"

"I don't know, do we only get one question per day?"

He glanced out the window, "I mean, we are making up the rules as we go, so I guess we could change them if needed."

"All in favor say 'Aye'," I raised my hand, "Aye."

Roland chuckled, this time the smile reached his eyes, brightening his entire countenance. I took another sip of wine and waited for his answer.

He cleared his throat. "I don't think I have as deep of thoughts as you do. I'm single, but that's more by choice."

"Oh?" I raised an eyebrow, thankful for the distraction to pull my emotions together. I should leave a large tip for the waitress—either that or steal the sodden napkin.

"I've just always had my mind set on a particular future and dating around hasn't been part of it. So, it's been my choice to avoid the memo."

I nodded slowly, wishing I had the strength to say those words. To say that all of this had been done by choice. And yet, how was I complaining? What an ungrateful person I could be. Here I was sitting in England, not paying a dime for travel or food, working a flexible business that I had started on my own, and yet, I had the gall to complain.

But that was the problem when something hurt—it simply hurt. Compared to where I was a few years ago, I was stronger and healed—but it was this new dig that had brought it all back to the surface.

Hope. Hope can be the hardest thing to kill, and yet, when pieces were taken away, I felt as though my breath had been sucked from my lungs. I'd hoped for something with Mason and it had crashed and burned. Not his fault. Not mine, or at least maybe I could have done something more, but it was done.

That door was slammed shut.

Glancing at Roland, I wondered what it must feel like to close that door on your own. To take control of your own emotions and make things happen.

"What did you mean when you told me to take a leap of faith?" I asked, bluntly.

Roland took a sip of his water and shrugged. "What did you think I meant?"

Flashes of courage ran through my mind. Me trying to tell Mason how I felt, and then this trip to England. "I took it as a seize the day."

He nodded. "I guess something like that. I meant for you to go for what you want."

"I wondered," I amended, and then added in a mumble, "too bad I'm cursed." I laughed and took a sip of wine, feeling it warm my belly. At Roland's curious look I explained, "My middle name."

His brow furrowed even further, "What, Charlotte?"

I nodded. "Danielle Charlotte Winthers."

"What's wrong with your middle name?"

I waved a hand in the air with abandon. "It's nothing really, just some silly thing I told myself years ago. I'm like Charlotte Lucas."

"From *Pride and Prejudice*?" he asked, looking at me as though I needed to have my head checked.

"Just a dumb thought. She's a spinster in the making," I pointed to myself, "and she gives quite the speech on being single and out of options."

"But you aren't out of options." He stated as though it was a matter of fact—almost angry.

"No," I sighed and looked out the window, "but I am afraid," I whispered the last bit to myself only to realize he'd heard. He was watching me with an intensity I'd never seen before. "I'm afraid of the future and of being alone."

He held my gaze and blinked, once, twice, and then shook his head. "You won't ever be alone." I swallowed around the lump in my throat. "You have your family and your friends."

"And you're my dearest friend," I admitted softly. I'd meant the words to be comforting, to affirm this bond we shared, but the intensity snapped and he looked away.

"Exactly," he sighed and ran a hand through his hair like he always did when he was frustrated and uncomfortable. I blinked, uncertain of what I'd done. "Well, shall we?" he asked.

The moment disappeared. I nodded.

Together, we shrugged on our coats and walked the short block back to the inn. The cold air awakened my senses, cutting through the fuzz of the wine and I suddenly realized how much I was leaning on Roland's arm. He seemed to hardly notice as we made our way up to our room, gently guiding me with his arm around my side.

"I think I had one glass too many," I said, feeling guilty. Normally I didn't let myself have more than a glass, but it had been so cozy and warm there.

"Here," Roland said as we reached the top of the staircase and entered our room. I was trying to take off my shoes when he guided me over to my bed and made me sit down. Kneeling on the floor his fingers worked quickly to undo the laces of my boots. I watched, knowing that those fingers, those hands, could create magic with the proper tools, a workbench, and some reclaimed wood.

His dark hair fell forward as he concentrated on slipping my foot out of the boot and then began to undo the laces of the other. Perhaps it was the shimmer of his hair in the dim light from the lamp or the mere fact that I had always wondered what his hair felt like, but I found myself mesmerized.

Reaching out, I placed my hand on his head and felt him still beneath me. Ever so slowly, he raised his chin, my boot was forgotten as he gazed up at me—the warmth in his eyes making my cheeks flush more than the wine. I laced my fingers through his hair, almost studying it. I could feel my breathing hitch and felt his hold too.

Finally, I met his gaze. There was a burning restraint in his eyes that I couldn't name.

"I'm afraid a lot of the time," I confessed, running my fingers through his hair once more, "but never when I'm with you."

Just like that, a cord was tied between us, a confirmation of the depth of feeling. I tested it, wondering how strong it was, and found that it had been there far longer than I realized, and it was tightly wound, built with strength. How had I never noticed how deeply bonded I was to him?

Roland closed his eyes and I watched his Adam's apple bob. We were standing on a precipice; I could feel it—this bond between us shifting. One choice to go forward, and one to retreat. I waited, wondering what he would decide and not knowing what I wanted. Instinct told me to flee.

With a soft sigh, Roland broke the spell. He looked back down and finished unlacing my boot. Though the spell was broken, the cord between our hearts remained tight.

He stood then, towering above me, and helped me beneath the covers. I was more than capable of standing on my own, but what was wrong with a helping hand? When the covers were tucked up around my chin as I liked them, he leaned down to place his hand on the side of my face.

My breath left me.

"When I'm with you, I'm not afraid either." He paused, opened his mouth, and then closed it. I desperately wanted to know what he was going to say. For some reason I knew it would change everything—and an undiscovered piece of me longed to hear it. But all too soon, the tremor of hope dissipated.

Roland smiled, almost mournfully, and sighed, his thumb brushing along my cheek. And just like that, I could see he had changed his mind. His words would remain a mystery.

"I had no idea you felt so alone," he murmured. When I softly smiled, he leaned down and placed a kiss on my forehead, so gentle and light that it felt like a butterfly's wings.

As I closed my eyes, I drifted, and suddenly I was asleep.

CHAPTER 14

It turns out that those glasses of wine helped me fall into a restful and much-needed sleep. So deep in fact that I awoke to the sound of the shower running and my mind had to play catch up to remember where I was.

Disorientation dissipated and with it, my cheeks flushed. I wasn't sure if I had ever been more honest in my life than I had been last night. It was at once exciting and terrifying.

The shower shut off and I glanced toward the door, knowing Roland was behind it. Choosing distraction, I reached for my phone and answered a few emails from clients. Most were simple questions and alterations that I could handle when I got back home.

Yawning, I saw a message from Mrs. Kent. She was asking for an update. I set a reminder in my phone to email her later. After spending one day at Chatsworth, I thought I finally had the essence of what she wanted for their Bed & Breakfast. It needed to center on a harmony of elegance and simplicity mingling in restful tranquility.

There were also a few messages from Anna asking for more details. I told her I would message later, a little uncertain of what all I could tell her. Could I even mention last night?

Stretching beneath the covers, I yawned again. The door to the bathroom opened with a loud crack, as though the paint was tacky. I curled back into a ball beneath the comforter.

Roland passed into my line of vision and I closed my eyes, not wanting to admit I was awake yet. Embarrassment seeped in. Had I actually run my fingers through his hair? Heat flooded my cheeks once more and I hoped he wouldn't notice.

I would never forget the look in his eyes as he gazed up at me, his hand on my foot. Even thinking of it now set my heart to pounding.

"Dani?" he whispered. So much for that. I internally cringed and anchored what little courage I had. Maybe we could both put a pin in last night and pretend it didn't happen.

I peeked one eye open, "Yes?" My voice came out groggier than I was expecting.

He laughed. "We need to get going if we want to meet Alexander on time." I grumbled, half agreement, half annoyance. "I can run down and grab something to eat while you change, or shower, or whatever."

Glancing up, I found him looking away, his hand twitching at his side as it did sometimes when he was nervous. So, he remembered last night as much as I did, however, he seemed to be choosing my method too. Maybe if we both ignored what happened, we could let it all go.

When he left the room, I sighed in relief. Without him nearby I could reorder my thoughts. I would be able to put Roland back in the box where he belonged, and I could rebuild my walls. I was so stupid to have answered him so honestly at dinner. I wouldn't let it happen again.

Showered and changed, I felt like a soldier returned to her fortress. This was nothing I couldn't handle. I was Dani, I could do this. And he was only Roland. *My friend, Roland.*

Last night could be dealt with at a different time. All I had done was touch his hair, that wasn't too weird, was it? Some friends did that. Yeah, it was nothing. It was fine. Totally fine.

As I threw on my coat and followed Roland out the door, I determined that none of this would get the better of me. Roland had only asked me those things to win the bet, and now it was my turn to gain some insight.

With that goal in mind, I knew I could remain focused on our friendship and put him back in that box. England was messing with my mind, and I intended to fight it.

The sighing hush of running water filled my ears, easing what little nerves I'd had during the climb. Upon reaching Chatsworth, Alexander had instructed us to climb a hill where the Cascade House rested at the top. Along the hill was a man-made fountain of sorts—steps with water gushing over the stone. We walked beside the cascading fountain, each step a little different from the next. In some places, there was a smooth surface before the stairs rose again. The result was a pleasant symphony of rushing water. Sometimes it trickled, other times it whispered, before falling heavily.

Apparently, luck was on our side. Alexander had said that only every now and then was the fountain on during the off-season. We seemed to have hit the right day for maintenance to be checking the pipes. Whatever it was, I was glad for it.

"I'm telling you," I said, "It's different!"

Roland stuck his head out awkwardly, his ear jutting forward, as though it would help him listen better. For all his creative abilities and acuteness to spotting a flaw in a piece of wood, he wasn't the best when it came to sounds.

"Yes, do that," I mimicked him, sticking out my neck. "That really helps you hear better."

He laughed, "I think it's working."

"You're ridiculous," I snorted and continued to climb, leaving him behind at one of the staircases. We were about halfway up the hill and thankfully the awkwardness of this morning had shifted as we settled back into the normalcy of our relationship. That was the nice part about friendship, it could alter and change, but the foundation was always a quiet resting place.

This here, laughing with him, enjoying comfortable silences, was where we'd learned to ground our friendship. I couldn't even count how many parties or gatherings we'd spent standing side by side, him holding a cup of water, me a soda, as we watched out for our friends.

"This has to have something to do with gravity and energy," Roland mumbled looking down the hill. "I'll have to ask Alexander if it ever powered the house."

Typical. I nearly rolled my eyes. He would be the one to think of the mechanics of the fountain rather than just enjoy its beauty. That's when I most liked to visit his shop. Most days he was building tables and chairs, bedroom suits, or dressers, but occasionally he would get the chance to make something truly creative. He told me once that it kept him interested and his skills acute.

It was only when he was working on something new that he seemed lost to the world. His mind was so focused on his hands and the wood beneath his fingers that he didn't even realize I was watching.

Smiling to myself, I studied him now. His hair stirred slowly in the breeze, his shoulders were broad and muscular beneath his jacket, toned from hours of hard work in his shop—not to mention the little weight room he had tacked onto the back of his store where his bedroom was located. How had I never noticed so many of these details about him? I'd always seen Mason so clearly. I flinched away from that thought.

"How come you've never bought a house?" I asked abruptly.

It took him a moment to answer, but he peered over his shoulder at me. "What made you think of that?"

I shrugged. "I don't know, I was just thinking."

"I guess I just haven't really thought about it."

"You haven't thought about it?" I queried, disbelieving. "Roland, you make enough money to probably pay for a house in cash. You could buy any house you wanted, live anywhere you wanted."

"And how would you know that?" He followed me the rest of the way up the hill. When we reached the top, we turned to look down on Chatsworth, the view was breathtaking.

"I do manage your website," I said, pushing my reluctant hair behind my ears. "I've seen the number of orders you get."

One side of his mouth lifted. "I get by."

"Understatement of the century."

He laughed. "Perhaps."

"Have you thought about hiring some help?"

"I did," he scratched his head. "Dave is actually working the shop right now." I stared up at him. Dave was a high school friend who'd moved away right after we graduated. I hadn't known he was back. I suddenly felt as though there were so many things I didn't know about Roland. "He's been helping with the basics of pieces, getting them ready for some of the finishing touches and whatnot."

"In other words, your professional touch."

Roland laughed and his cheeks flushed slightly with color. Did I just embarrass him? I wasn't sure if I had ever done that before.

"Something like that."

"I didn't realize you'd hired Dave."

He shrugged. "It was a quick decision. I'm also training Cole to work the table saw, his mom wants him to learn a trade, something to fall back on even though he gets straight A's. It's good to know how to do something with your hands."

I nodded, he'd told me that before. "Were we ever tough on you for that?"

"For what?"

"For staying in Landing and working your way through college online. I know Joel teased you about it a lot."

"Ahh," he shrugged. "Joel is Joel."

"But we still teased you." I thought back to that night with the bonfire and trampoline. Was our teasing a cause of his sadness? We had all been leaving for college and he was staying in Landing. Had I been a bad friend? Biting my lip, I wondered if I could ask him about that night.

"It was fine, Dani. There's no reason for you to be concerned. Trust me." He looked down at me, "I did plenty of teasing too."

"Okay, well, if I ever said anything to hurt you, I'm sorry."

He shook his head. "You never hurt me with your teasing."

That phrase was worded very carefully. I peered up at him as he turned around to view the Cascade House at the top of the fountain. I wanted to be interested in the architecture and design, but I couldn't get those words out of my mind. Had I hurt him in some way?

Again, the image of that tear escaping his eye came back to my mind. It was a memory that had always bothered me, but to wonder now if I was the cause of it, made it all the worse.

"Shall we?" Roland asked, breaking into my thoughts. He waved toward the great house beneath us.

"I guess so, Alexander is probably tired of waiting in the cold."

"Oh, I think it would take more than this to make that man tired."

I laughed. Roland was right. The man was a bundle of unspent energy and mirth—and in my opinion, every tour guide should be held to the "Alexander-Standard". He didn't know it, but all future tour guides would be measured against him from now on. I just might have to tell him, I'm sure he would get a kick out of it.

"You still haven't answered my question about a house," I pointed out as we traipsed back down the hill, digging my hands into the pockets of my coat for warmth.

"Oh, right," he hesitated. "Well, I just don't need a lot of space. All I really do is work, and help out at the church. There's no need for me to have a mortgage right now, other than the store."

I nodded. He was always so logical, methodical. He'd been a huge help when I first moved into my loft. He and my dad had fixed the stairs, the door jams, faucets, and my garbage disposal. As long as I paid him with Baker's Local Deli sandwiches, he didn't seem to mind.

"Hmm," was all I said.

"What was that?"

"What?"

"That, *hmm*."

"I don't know, I was just thinking."

He nudged my shoulder. "You're always thinking."

"Creative mind," I sighed, dramatically flipping back my hair.

"Ahh, it's not just that. You hide a lot of yourself from the world, you always have."

So quickly he was able to disarm me, to surge over my walls. My heart seemed to stutter, wondering why I had never noticed his ability to cut to the heart of a matter before. Rallying, I reminded myself that I was supposed to be getting to him—to winning this bet. Even though the bet seemed further and further from reality.

"You're not an open book either," I managed.

When he didn't respond, I found him watching me, his brow furrowed as though in confusion. He seemed to want to say something but thought better of it.

"See, like that." I waved toward him. "You always rethink what you want to say. What were you just now going to ask me?"

"You really want to know?" he paused on the hill—we were nearly to the bottom.

I nodded, biting my lip.

He took a deep breath. "I was wondering if you thought Mason was an open book."

That took me by surprise. Where had that thought come from?

"Mason?"

"Come on Dani, I've seen the way you look at him."

Disarmed, again. Our unspoken contract was crumbling.

I ran a hand through my hair, glancing right and left. "What are you actually asking me?" I raised my chin, almost certain I knew where this was headed.

"Do you still want him?"

A lump formed in my throat—panic setting in. Hadn't I cried all the tears for Mason? Hadn't I put it all to rest?

"I don't know." The words were barely audible.

Meeting Roland's gaze was one of the hardest things I had ever done because I knew what I would see there. And sure enough, I saw it—the sharp gleam that broke through all my pretenses. So many times he'd given me this look, it was comfort and protection amid my raging fears. He always offered it to me freely, steadying the turmoil in my heart. But right now, it didn't seem to hold me. It disarmed me in a way that bared my heart to the world. I wanted to run away, to tuck it all aside.

He waited patiently for me to gather my thoughts. He was always waiting for me.

"I did," I admitted. "I wanted the idea of him." Some of the weight fell off my chest. "I hoped for something with him for years. That night," I waved a hand, "I was going to tell him."

Roland nodded as though this confirmed something. He looked away and I watched as the English breeze lifted the strands of his hair around his ears. They were slightly pink at the tips from the cold.

Saying the truth out loud helped. For what felt like the first time in a long time, I took a deep breath that filled my lungs.

"Can I tell you what I think?" Roland asked, his voice deep, almost a grumble.

I didn't answer but just waited.

"I think you deserve someone who understands you." It was an odd phrase, one he seemed to have thought many times. "You should be with someone who isn't going to hold you back." His honesty was like a punch to my gut.

"And you think Mason would?"

He scoffed and started walking down the hill again. "I like Mason, but he is clueless to anything outside of his own life goals."

My brow furrowed; I had never really heard Roland criticize anyone before. "I'll keep that in mind," I mumbled. "Not that it really matters though, he's dating Nancy."

"But it does if you're still wanting to be with him."

"I don't know what I am anymore."

"Maybe that's a good thing," he said. "It gives you the freedom to figure out what you want. A new dream."

I glanced up. As brutal as it was, I liked this new way we talked. How had I not realized the relief that came with the truth? It was so seamless, as though it had always been lingering there in the fog waiting to be discovered.

"What did you think?" Alexander shouted from the gravel pathway, still fifty yards away.

The tension cleared. "Beautiful!" I called back.

We could see Alexander's head already bobbing and I picked up my pace, certain he would have all kinds of stories for me about the fountain. Sure enough, he launched into details about the mechanics and answered all of Roland's questions about its purpose. He'd been right about it being used as a source of power.

I slightly tuned Alexander out as we walked back toward the house, my thoughts running through what Roland had said. Was it possible that he didn't think Mason and I wouldn't fit together? And why was that?

It stung to think my best friend didn't see what I saw, and yet, I couldn't help wondering if I had been wrong all along. It was true I often didn't see myself the way others did—I had been told this many times—but I felt certain I knew what I wanted. *But did I?*

Thinking of Mason now, I tested my feelings. He was still there, lingering, but the dream of a future was fading. It had been ripped out and in its place was simply a friend. Perhaps my eyes had been cleared and reality had settled. Like a sandy cloud in an ocean wave, the tide had pulled back and I could finally see.

Maybe Mason and I were never meant to be. The thought yanked painfully on my heart and I wondered if I had wasted my years. Blinking, I came out of my reverie as Alexander's voice changed. He leaned in and his eyebrows waggled as he whispered.

"Now, have you ever heard of the mystery of the letters written in blood?"

And just like that, he had my attention. I smiled, hanging onto his every word as we transitioned back into the house, all the while wondering if I could take any more discoveries.

CHAPTER 15

Where the first tour had been fascinating, the second tour with Alexander was illuminating. He delved deeper into the rooms, sharing stories that built on what he'd told us the day before.

There is something about watching a person with passion in their environment. They light up, their faces glowing as they speak of the thing that excites them most. And sometimes, a person didn't even have to speak. Roland hardly ever spoke about his carpentry, but I'd been privy to his process. Many times, when I'd arrived at lunch he would still be working, his hands guiding a table saw. I'd watch him, my eyes focusing on his face. It was there in the lines of his mouth, in the careful way his eyes moved and the energy of his arms that I saw his passion. He loved what he did, and it was the only place I ever saw him unrestrained.

For a long time, I'd noticed how he often seemed to be holding something back. As though pieces of himself wouldn't be accepted.

Thinking of what he'd said by the Cascade House, I wondered if we had teased him too much in high school. That summer before college had been a whirlwind. A time of making memories while also looking ahead to the horizon and all that was new.

We'd spent hours talking about the new friends and experiences we would make. It had been that time when we thought we were invincible—seniors in a small town, ready to take on the world. Running a hand through my hair, I laughed at that old Danielle. She'd thought she knew what life would throw her. But nothing had come out the way I expected.

That was the year I hoped Mason would finally see me as the grown woman I was. I'd thought that when we finally saw each other at Christmastime he would notice me. I'd spent that first semester keeping up with him on social media, only to meet his new girlfriend at Christmas.

Of course, by the following year, that relationship had crashed and burned. Mason had turned to me and Kari to help him through it. Then he was on to the next girl and the ensuing breakup. How many times had that happened over the last eight years? Too many to count.

If there was one area in which I wish Mason would change, it was his constant pursuit of relationships. Maybe that was why it hurt more when he didn't see me as an option. He didn't seem all that picky.

"Come now, Dani," Alexander's voice echoed across the room. He tapped his walking canes in impatience. I sped to catch up, crossing the long hallway and toward the white stone doorway where he stood with Roland.

Alexander had taken to calling me Dani when he'd heard Roland shorten my name. Normally it would bother me, but not here. Somehow, in the short time we'd known him, Alexander had become a dear friend.

There was one thing I noticed about growing up, and that is at times it was more difficult to make friends. Not because of differences, but because of a will to keep others at a distance. By my age, I had selected my closest friends and it was difficult to let another person in. But when I did, they became part of my closest circle.

Alexander led the way forward, and I gasped when we stepped into a stone room. My hand flew to my mouth and I stared, wide-eyed. Alexander laughed and flourished his canes while shouting with glee, "Surprise! I saved the best for last!"

I didn't want to admit I was close to tears, but I was. I swallowed heavily a smile spreading over my lips. I had completely forgotten about this place.

The sculpture room.

There I was, standing like Elizabeth Bennet, all agog at the sculptures before me. All sound fell away and it was as though I could hear the piano playing gently in the background, the soft notes filtering through my mind as I began to explore.

How had Alexander known that this was one of my favorite scenes? I'd even written a term paper on it in college, comparing this scene to the portrait Elizabeth witnesses in the book. I'd compared the sensuality of the sculptures to an awakening in Elizabeth. I'd proposed that the rising of her emotions and interest in Mr. Darcy was more profound when she stood before the bust of the very man she had denied, rather than a portrait.

My hand was covering my mouth as I slowly stepped into the room. I was aware of Alexander's laugh, but it faded as my gaze roved over each sculpture in turn. From the *Sleeping Lion* to the *Recumbent Bacchante*, each so intricately detailed and smooth that I wanted to reach out and touch the sculptures. Instead, I safely tucked my hands into the pockets of my coat.

There was as much curiosity here as what I fancied Elizabeth must have felt. There was a beckoning of discovery that moved me through the room, and a stillness that allowed me to appreciate the forms and craftsmanship. From sculpture to sculpture I moved, pausing at the *Vestal Virgin* where a veil shrouded her face. How did the artist make marble appear like a veil? It was incredible.

From somewhere in the back of my mind, the gentle theme from the movie began to play from memory. I was at peace here. Only when I turned did my eyes widen in surprise.

There he was.

Mr. Darcy in all his finery—the bust from the movie stood off to the side. Walking forward, I remained at a slight distance and stared. It was quite the depiction of Matthew McFayden, and it looked exactly as it had in the movie. I don't know why I thought it would look any different.

Like everything here, it was too real, too raw, and I didn't know if I wanted to examine it any closer.

"Is it a true likeness?"

I was jolted from my reverie to see Roland standing beside me. But he wasn't looking at the bust, instead, his eyes were carefully trained on me—a smirk curving one side of his mouth.

"I knew you'd seen *Pride and Prejudice* more than once."

He laughed, the sound low and intimate, "I never said I hadn't. I told you it's my mom's favorite movie."

"I'm starting to think it is yours."

He cocked his head to the side as though calculating the craftsmanship of the piece. I knew he was only trying to humor me. "Careful," he pointed to a little sign on the side, "they probably have cameras."

I leaned forward to see what he was talking about. My eyes were never quite as good as his.

Sure, enough the sign on the pedestal holding the bust read. *Please do not kiss.*

I placed a hand over my mouth, smirking. "You know what's the best part about that?"

"That it had to happen multiple times before they put up a sign?"

"Exactly!" I broke into laughter again and moved closer to look at the sign. "I mean, who does that?"

Roland had his phone out and when I blew Mr. Darcy a kiss, I heard the sound of his camera click. "That should cost you a fine," he chuckled and I shrugged.

"Worth it," I winked at him and felt his gaze follow me as I looked around the room in awe. "This is just amazing." I didn't expect him to answer, but he did anyway.

"Take your time."

All laughter had disappeared from those eyes of his, and a look I hadn't seen before entered his gaze. It was warm, heated almost, and his darkened pupils roved over my face before he abruptly turned and left me beside Mr. Darcy. The suddenness was like the shock of cold morning air after warm blankets were cast aside. It was startling and took a moment to adjust.

Watching him walk away, my eyes drifted lower, watching the lithe way he moved. The muscles in his legs and along with his… I cut the thought short.

Pull yourself together, Dani.

I turned and began to make a loop around the room. Alexander and Roland were conversing behind me on a bench, but I ignored them as I attempted to flush out the color from my cheeks. But each new statue seemed to remind me of what I had done—of what I had been looking at.

I was flushed again and it didn't help that I was surrounded by naked sculptures. All around me was rounded flesh and smooth muscle.

Biting my lip, I wondered about Charlotte Lucas as though she was a real person. Had she at any point been drawn to a man? She had to have been—hadn't she? But I couldn't possibly see how she was drawn to Mr. Collins. Perhaps there had been someone else, but she had been too cowardly to try. It's too bad Jane Austen hadn't written the true life and dreams of Charlotte Lucas.

Feeling as though I was sweating, I turned from the bust of Napoleon, hoping to view something as simple as the *Sleeping Lion*. Instead, laying before me was a naked man grasping his heel—*Achilles Wounded*. My eyes widened and I swallowed. For goodness sake, I was twenty-seven years old. It wasn't as if I'd never seen a naked man before.

Flashes of college parties and streaking boys ran through my mind, only to fade all too quickly. But it wasn't the nakedness that had reached me, it was the pain in the man's face—the look of pure agony for he knew his heel was his greatest weakness. I knew weakness all too well.

Pulling myself together, I turned, determined to be better—to for once channel my inner-Charlotte and not let anything bother me. I had a choice here and these statues, although sensual, were just mere representations of some model. I pushed back all thoughts of what they emulated, or what the artist was trying to convey. It was just marble.

I nearly cursed when I turned around again. There was *Sleeping Endymion*. Was this entire room filled with nearly naked men?

Well aware that Roland and Alexander could see me, I carefully pretended I was reading the plaque accompanying the statue. I knew the myth of Endymion well, how Selene, the goddess of the moon, had fallen in love with him and asked Zeus to grant him eternal youth. Zeus had complied, but also cursed him with eternal sleep—and this was the result.

My eyes roved over the carefully constructed form of well-muscled masculinity. He was sleeping peacefully, his arm cocked behind his head and a cloth covering part of his waist and leg. The rest of him remained exposed, and as I stared, he was so life-like that I almost expected him to take a breath.

As though from awakening, I remembered watching Roland sleep. The gentle rise and fall of his chest. Idly, I wondered what it would be like to sleep beside him, to wake up to his heavy arm around my waist.

Staring at the sculpture now, I knew my cheeks were flushed. I'd felt as though I'd intruded on a private moment that night, and right now it seemed as though I was betraying our friendship to even think of Roland in that way.

Turning, I forced my heart to slow. Never in my life had I thought of Roland in such a way, and now, twice in one afternoon I'd stared at his backside and fancied the memory of him asleep.

I needed air.

"Hey."

"Ahh!" I shouted, my voice echoing off the walls.

Roland was staring down at me, his brow furrowed slightly. "Are you ready to go? Alexander said something about having a date in the village." His lips quirked into a grin.

"A date?" I blinked. My mind so far elsewhere it was taking a moment to gather my bearings.

Roland continued to stare. "Yes, something about a woman he's been seeing. She's a lucky gal."

"Oh," was all I could manage. I ran a hand through my hair, pretending that my heart wasn't beating out of my chest. I'd never been like this with Roland before. My hands were shaking. "Yes, let's go."

"All right then," he was still staring, but at least he no longer looked confused. "Let's," he waved a hand for me to move toward Alexander and the exit beyond. I was thankful for the excuse to walk in front of him—at least that way I wouldn't catch myself staring at his backside.

Shaking my head, I knew I was done for.

CHAPTER 16

"Please keep in touch," Alexander said, waving his phone. He'd just given me his email address.

I smiled. "We will, and hopefully someday we can come back."

"When you do, come in the Spring it is beautiful."

"I don't know," I said, "this has been so wonderful."

"It's not every day you get a private tour," Alexander winked, shifting his weight on his canes.

Roland stuck out his hand to shake Alexander's, thanking him for everything he'd done for us over the past two days.

"Ah," he shook the compliments away, "No need to thank me. It was my pleasure. Just take care of this one," he gave me an extra squeeze. I blushed. "It's not every day we move the Mr. Darcy bust to the Sculpture Room."

"What?" I asked. "It's not usually there?"

"Not at all, he's usually in the gift shop. But I had him moved." He laughed as though enjoying a private joke. "I wanted to see the full effect and you didn't disappoint."

I laughed and shook my head, embarrassed down to my toes. I didn't even know what to say.

We exchanged final goodbyes and promises to keep in touch.

"Well," Roland said as we rolled over the hills leaving Chatsworth behind us. I was staring out the back window until we rounded the final curve and it disappeared.

"Yeah," I sighed, a sadness creeping in.

"I was wondering something."

"What's that?"

"Have you ever wanted to go to Scotland?"

I blinked, staring at him. He glanced my way, one hand on the steering wheel, the other resting along the window. "Seriously?"

"I asked my Nan and she said the roads should be clear enough. We can stay with them for a week before I have to get back to my shop. I wasn't sure what your schedule looked like—but they have Wi-Fi so you could do some work…" he trailed off.

A lightness entered me. Just when I had thought this was all over, we were about to embark on something new. *Scotland.*

I'd always wanted to go. The cautious side of my brain sent a warning about all the work I needed to get done. But the other part cast all resistance to the wind.

I couldn't stop the smile that spread across my lips. "Let's do it."

Roland grasped my hand and squeezed my fingers, "Onward!"

I laughed knowing my walls were continuing to crumble, but for the first time in a long time, I didn't mind in the least.

———————————

The glow from the dashboard was dimmed by the white flecks swirling before the headlights of the car. I was leaning over the steering wheel, driving slower than I ever had in my life, peering as though life itself depended on it.

Worrying my lower lip, I squinted into the blustering snowflakes. *Not good.*

We'd spent one more night in Bakewell. Just long enough to enjoy some time at a local pub, and contact our families to let them know our plans. My mother had been particularly happy to know that Roland was with me. I tried not to let that sink in too far. Even Anna had asked how my heart was…I'd yet to answer her.

It was all I could do to contain my excitement after Roland showed me a picture of Gairloch, the village where his grandparents lived. It was quite a drive, nine and a half hours to be exact. But nothing we couldn't handle.

Roland had agreed to split driving duties with me. He'd taken the first shift since I tended to move slowly in the morning and the last thing I needed to be doing while tired was driving on the left side of the road.

Of course, I hadn't factored in the other part of that equation—that I would be driving when night fell. Internally cursing, I kicked up the windshield wipers another notch. It didn't feel like they were doing much.

Roland was asleep in the passenger seat, I only knew because I heard his deep breaths. They were the only thing keeping me sane. I was scared—I'd never driven in snow and to learn now, while driving on the wrong side of the road, and at night, was not my idea of fun.

Taking a calming breath for what seemed like the millionth time, I kept my hands glued to the steering wheel. This really shouldn't be that difficult, I could handle it.

As though taunting me with its charm, the stone wall along the left side of the car gave way to a slim, and weak guard rail. Beyond was a glimmering shadow. One glance at the GPS in the dashboard told me we were now driving beside a loch.

"Perfect," I muttered under my breath. I had a bad feeling about all of this.

Headlights flashed in the rearview mirror and I let one curse go. It slipped from my lips as though it had been waiting on my tongue for a long time.

Either my eyes were tired or the idiot behind me had his bright lights on, but whatever it was, I could hardly see. I cursed and cursed again, this time a little louder.

The wind wipers snapped back and forth to near exhaustion and I wondered if it was possible to bend a steering wheel.

I hate this. I hate this. I hate this.

If only there was someplace to pull over, I could let this crazed driver behind me pass and take a moment to gather myself. But there was nothing. Just trees, this skinny winding road, and a sheer drop on Roland's side that plunged into a loch. We were done for.

I couldn't see more than ten feet in front of me as the snowflakes began to fall harder as though taunting me and my fears. I could have cursed the skies, and then when the driver behind me swerved to the other side of the road to pass, a foul word rang through the car.

Maybe it was fear, or maybe it was the first drop in a tidal wave that had been held back for too long, but after that one word, curses began to flow in a torrent with more volume than I intended.

They were interspersed with me shouting, "Oh I hate this!" before the cursing began again.

An oncoming car's lights blinded me and I thought we were done for. One giant curse and it was all I could do to keep the tears at bay.

"Dani."

I screamed and the car swerved slightly. I'd completely forgotten about Roland in my panic. "Sorry!" I shouted. "I just, this is awful. Oh, I hate it, I just hate it!" And more curses. I'd never been like this in my life.

"Okay, okay, calm down," Roland sounded like he was about to laugh.

"This is not funny!" I yelled—fear lacing my voice.

"I know it's not," his voice was strained and I knew if I looked at him I would see the humor in his eyes. He was barely containing his laughter.

"I'm serious Roland," I shouted, panicked "This is so not funny!"

"Okay, okay, just relax." He was a little more in control. "Take a deep breath. You're a great driver, just keep your eyes on the road and we'll find a place to pull over, and then I can drive the rest of the way."

"Okay, okay," I mimicked. This is what I needed, a voice of reason to keep me on course. "Does this thing show you a place to stop?" I jabbed at the digital map in the dashboard.

"I don't think so."

A white sign flashed up ahead and my annoyance flared. "Also, what the—" and I said a word I wasn't proud of, "—is with that sign?!"

Roland read in a voice that nearly cracked with laughter, "Oncoming vehicles in the middle of the road."

"Like what am I supposed to do?! Do we get hit head-on and it's okay because the sign told us it might happen?" I was shouting in desperation.

"That's a possibility." Roland was laughing at me, or at least trying not to, and failing miserably. "At least they won't have a guilty conscience."

"Roland Harmon, so help me I will strangle you when I get out of this car."

He laughed then, and loudly. The sound dulled out the violent snapping of the wipers, and when he snorted, I began to chuckle. The tension eased slowly as we continued onward and into the dark of the Scottish Highlands. If only I had remembered how it got dark so quickly here. It was only six o'clock and already looked as dark as midnight.

Rounding a curve, I took a deep breath and wiped at the tears that were now threatening my vision too. "We're going to die," I said under my breath and Roland completely lost it. His booming laugh filled the car, so contagious I couldn't stop myself.

Roland slapped at his leg, breathless. "Oh!" he said and then his shoulders shook again. "That was hilarious!" I choked out a sound and wiped at the tears rolling down my cheeks. "I had no idea you could curse like that," he gasped.

I bit my lip, snorting too. "I didn't either." Another bout of laughter followed—I clung to the steering wheel for breath.

Eventually, we both sighed, the laughter slowing and Roland saying, "Oh man," now and then as we both gathered ourselves. My stomach hurt and I figured my mascara had run down my face. Shaking my head, I took a calming breath and let myself focus on the road.

"There's your favorite sign," Roland pointed. "On the bright side, we only have about twenty minutes until we're there."

"Really?"

"Yes, I think you can make it."

"I think so," I smiled, determined.

No sooner had I said the words, then we rounded a curve, and as if in slow motion I saw a bridge, less than ten feet away. And on that bridge was a truck. There was nowhere to go but forward.

I didn't have time to register what was happening, or maybe I did because rather than the normal human reaction of slamming on the breaks, I panicked, my foot slamming the accelerator to the car floor. The car shot forward like a child snapped on the backside with a rubber band. Eyes wide, I screamed as Roland slammed his hand into the ceiling as though it would help.

The lights came closer and I could only imagine what the driver in the truck might have seen, two wide-eyed adults, terrified for their lives—mouths open in horrified screams. We shot past, somehow missing the truck as Roland yelled, "Holy Sh—!"

The truck flew by, missing us by mere inches. We flew off the bridge and I pulled my foot from the gas pedal in astonishment—shocked to not be seeing angels and white lights. Slowly, the car crept to a halt.

Our breaths became the only sound.

Gulping for air, I spotted a pull-off on the side of the road. Only the slightest touch of the pedal brought us to our new resting place. My heart thudded painfully in my chest, as I put the car in park.

I turned. All it took was one look at Roland, his hand still braced on the roof of the car, his mouth hanging open in astonishment, and I snorted. The most unladylike-cackle overwhelmed my ears and I couldn't stop. Oh, how my stomach hurt, but all I could hear was Roland cursing again and again under his breath. I tried to talk and couldn't breathe, only gasping for air.

"That was—" I inhaled sharply "—the funniest—thing I've"—breathing was too difficult, I clutched my stomach, "—ever heard!"

"Not funny, Dani," he shook his head, but his lips slowly quirking in wry humor.

"Not funny?! That was hysterical!" I threw my head back and tried to calm my breaths—and failed. "Roland Harmon actually cursed!"

I smacked his shoulder. He was laughing with me now. "I thought we were going to die."

"Me too!" I said and pressed my lips together looking at him. When his eyes met mine, we both lost it again. For how long we laughed I wasn't sure, but all I knew was my abs were going to be sore, my nose was running and my eyes had leaked enough tears for black mascara to come away on my fingers.

"Oh," I said, still clutching my stomach. "Do you want to drive the rest of the way?"

"I think that's necessary if we want to live," he chuckled and opened his door. I followed and walked out into the freezing night air, my cheeks growing sticky as though ice clung to them.

Taking a deep breath, I was about to hand the keys to him, when he beckoned me closer to the guard rail. "Come here." His voice had completely changed, a hint of wonder lingering in its depths.

"What?"

"Listen."

We grew quiet. Perhaps after driving so long in the dark, my eyes had adjusted, allowing me to see a bright moon shimmering across the surface of what looked like black ice. I knew it wasn't ice, but instead water with depths that mystified the mind and enticed imagination. Inhaling deeply through my nose, the sharp wind stung my nostrils. Never before had I felt such complete tranquility—or rather seen it.

"It's so quiet, and beautiful," I murmured, watching the snowflakes drift down around us. They had seemed so urgent while I was driving, a torrent of snow, but now they had relaxed, almost dancing upon the wind.

"A world of its own," Roland whispered.

I glanced up at him, his shoulder brushed against mine as he placed his hands in the pockets of his jacket. My heart stuttered slightly. Suddenly, I was very aware of how tall Roland was—I wanted to lean toward him, but that was a wall I shouldn't cross. The memory of the way I had run my fingers through his hair had me blushing.

"I think this view might prove you wrong."

He inclined his head. "What do you mean?"

I sighed, smiling softly as the clouds parted and we were covered in soft moonlight. Scrunching my toes inside my warm boots, I exhaled, watching the cloud of my breath dissipate before answering. "You said you were going to prove my heart belonged in England. I think Scotland may have been a better guess."

He met my gaze with the full force of his eyes—the intensity had returned.

It was the kind of look that could warm a person, the kind that held for what felt like minutes but was only a few seconds. One side of his mouth lifted, the moonlight playing over his face, snowflakes clinging to his dark hair, and I stared in wonder. At that moment I hoped I could forever remember him like this. His features illuminated faintly in the moonlight, his eyes drawing me in, and that smile. Oh, how had I never noticed how sweet his smile was? So gentle, so warm.

In his eyes was the kindness that came from a heart that sought to love others. It was a look I knew well, one that could focus on a person as though they were the only thing that mattered in the world.

My mouth opened slightly as I watched his gaze drift across my face. Inhaling, the Scottish air seemed to freeze my lungs. I blinked, adjusting when his eyes met mine once more—his gaze intent as though longing for me to read something in their depths.

Heart thundering, I sucked in another breath. I was on that wall of uncertainty again—perched and ready to fall one way or another. The only problem was I didn't know which way would be best. I wanted to stay on the wall—it was safer.

Shuddering a breath, I broke our gaze and turned to look back out over the water. Had Charlotte Lucas felt like this? This inner unrest which stirred up all her fears.

I could see something so clearly now—I could see Roland. All that was once our relationship had shifted, but I wasn't ready to acknowledge it. I didn't want things to change.

Maybe something like that had happened to Charlotte. It was pleasant to think that perhaps she'd had had a caller or two. That someone had doted on her. But why then had she chosen to marry Mr. Collins?

Pursing my lips, I ignored the warmth that seemed to radiate from Roland and remained focused on the water. Somehow, someway, I would overcome this fear. I wouldn't retreat and turn my life into something less than desirable because I was afraid. I would jump from the wall, but to what I didn't know.

Pulling the keys out of my pocket, they jingled in the night, their sound almost harsh in all that was quiet and still around us.

"Are you ready?" I asked, without looking up. I didn't want to read the words in his eyes. And even as I thought of what it all might mean, I wondered if I wanted him to say those words.

"Sure," Roland said, a hint of what had passed between us lingering in his voice. "We are almost there."

"Let's get going then," I said, trying to keep my voice level. In all reality, I was excited to meet his grandparents, but the emotions coursing through me had knocked me off-kilter.

Without another word, Roland started the car and guided us into the night.

CHAPTER 17

"There it is," Roland said, smiling.

A glowing lamp flickered along a stone wall as we rounded a curve in the road. The trees had long since parted and nothing but pitch darkness stretched out to the horizon—as if it could even be seen.

The outlines of a shadowed cottage formed—a husky white in the snow. Most of the windows on the lower floor were illuminated with lamps and the effect was inviting, like the warm sigh of a stoked hearth.

"I thought you said they live near the ocean."

"They do," Roland chuckled, "the ocean is just behind the house."

"Oh," I said, peering even harder through the windshield wipers, which were still snapping back and forth against the snow.

No sooner had the engine turned off than the front door opened. I smiled as a tall, elderly man made his way across the gravel drive toward us. Curious, I exited the car and watched him move in for a hug with Roland. Although a few inches shorter, I could tell where Roland had gotten his height.

Roland's childhood had been very different than mine. While my childhood had included an older brother and sister, Roland had been an only child, with just his mother to raise him. I'd asked him once if he ever saw his dad, but he'd just shaken his head and not brought up the topic again.

Throughout high school, I'd met Roland's mom, and she made the best lemon bars I'd ever tasted, but there were never any pictures of his father. I'd always wondered what he looked like, or which side of the family Roland took after. It seemed that the men on his mother's side had strong genes.

"Ahh, this must be Dani!" his grandfather smiled, his arms open wide for a hug. The embrace was warm and comforting, with an extra tight squeeze that made me feel more than welcome. I smiled up at this man I'd heard so much about, noting the lines around his eyes and the deep creases near his mouth. Would Roland ever have lines like that?

"Thank you for having me," I said, suddenly realizing I didn't know how to address him. All Roland had ever called him was Pap.

"It's a pleasure to finally meet you." There was a slight lilt in his voice, a proper English accent that reminded me of Alexander. "Roland, let me help you with the bags."

I reached out a hand, "Careful, it's heavy." I watched, self-conscious that my bag was too much, but he seemed unconcerned by the weight.

Their home was everything you could want in a quaint, seaside cottage. The inner décor so scattered and varied to the point it matched. Cozy rugs covered the creaking, wood floors, soft blankets were cast over a worn leather armchair and tan couch, while faint lamps lit the living room with a pleasant glow. Along the walls were so many pictures—oceans and valleys, subways and railcars, mountains and famous landmarks all scattered throughout the room. There seemed to be no order to them. Each one was an adventure and I was certain there were plenty of stories to go along with them. In some of the pictures Roland's grandparents appeared to be in their twenties, others in their middle-aged years, and the clearer images were more recent. I loved them all and crossed my arms as I perused the photos.

A few of them depicted a familiar face and I grinned looking at Roland standing between his grandparents, a gawky middle-schooler with braces. This was before I had met him, leaning closer I could see the strong chin of the man I now knew, though it was hidden in adolescent rounded cheeks. His nose was the same as ever.

"Making discoveries?" Roland asked, near my shoulder. I turned and smiled up at him.

"This was before I knew you," I said, wondering why I whispered. "Was this during a Christmas vacation?"

He shook his head. "No," he adjusted the suitcase he still held in his hand, "I spent a year in middle school living in England with Nan and Pap."

"Oh?" I had never heard this. "How come?"

He opened his mouth, about to say something when a woman's voice called down the hallway. "Roland!"

The woman who stepped in the doorway of the living room was every bit as petite as Roland's Pap was tall. Lines creased her brow and the crinkles around her eyes when she smiled seemed almost ingrained. She threw her arms open wide and hurried to embrace her grandson, nearly disappearing as he hugged her.

"Hey, Nan."

I couldn't help smiling, I loved this side of Roland. I had always appreciated the way he treated his mother. A good man knew how to be gentle with a woman.

"And this is…?" she clasped her hands together and beamed at me. Remembering how Pap had called me Dani, I realized Roland must always refer to me that way.

"I'm Dani," I said. It was the first time I'd ever introduced myself as such. Roland grinned behind his Nan's shoulder. Did he realize it too? He must call me Dani to them, and I was surprised to realize I wanted them too. Maybe my name across the pond would simply be Dani.

Roland's Nan opened her arms wide and hugged me, she barely reached my shoulders and I felt like a giant beside her. Was this how Roland always felt with me?

"Have you had something to eat?"

"Yes, ma'am."

"Oh," she glanced over her shoulder at Roland. "There are those southern manners. I remember when he visited after his first year in the South. He couldn't stop saying, 'ma'am' and 'sir.'" She laughed at the memory. "Please call me Nan."

Her smile was as quaint and welcoming as their cottage. I realized now that this place was every bit a reflection of her. Just one glance around the room and you could tell this couple valued people and memories, and here before me, they stood with an open invitation for me to join them.

I smiled. "I would like that."

Roland's mom had never been like this. Although she was always pleasant around me, she had never radiated this kind of warmth before. I suddenly realized that Roland had never seemed to fit with his mother, that I had always wondered where his genuine friendliness had come from. Now I knew.

It was odd their daughter wasn't like them, but maybe that was why she lived so far away from her parents. Not that I was complaining, otherwise I never would have met Roland.

Dinner was a quick affair, a warm stew already waiting for us on the stove. Nan served our bowls and as we all sat down to eat Pap asked us about our trip to Chatsworth. They laughed at our stories of Alexander, saying that he was always so friendly.

"He's been there for eighteen years, did he tell you that?" Pap said, grabbing a piece of the crusted bread that rested in the middle of the table. Though his wife had shaken her head twice, saying they had already eaten, she still smiled at him. I enjoyed being welcomed into this home. After so many years of hearing about them, I now got to know what they sounded like, how they talked, but there were so many things Roland had left out. He hadn't told me about the sweet way Nan patted his arm now and then, as though reminding herself he was truly there. Or how when his Pap laughed, his shoulders shook in little shrugs toward his ears, making him appear childlike for the blink of a moment.

Stories of far-off places and long-gone memories flowed through the night. As the glasses of wine flushed my cheeks, I blinked deeply—the journey through the snow long forgotten. Much later when I crept up the stairs, I found my hand sliding along the railing as the wood creaked beneath my feet. I loved this place. The welcoming, heartwarming home was as much a piece of Nan and Pap's lives as it was Roland's heart.

He followed me up the stairs as Nan led the way to where I would be staying. The door was just to the left of the landing and she scuttered around the bed, pulling out heavy blankets to fight off the chill of the room. My bag already sat on the chair along the wall.

"Do you think you will be warm enough?" Nan asked over her shoulder.

"It's perfect," I said, shoving down a shiver. It was slightly cold in the room, but the kind of cold that told me I would sleep well. A Christmas morning, holding a warm cup of coffee, kind of cold. I was already looking forward to climbing beneath the quilts.

"These are beautiful, did you make them?" I ran my hand over the fabric. My mom dappled in sewing and I could spot a quality piece. These looked handstitched.

"Oh, no!" Nan laughed. "My friend, Ilene, made these quilts. Lives just on the other side of town. Best quilts I've ever seen or used, and you know I've been around the world a time or two. If you put me down in front of a sewing machine all I could do is stare at it." She laughed to herself and placed her boney hands on her slim hips meeting my gaze. "Well, I think that's it, if you need anything else, we are just downstairs. Or you can bother Roland, he knows where everything is." She beamed at me and I heard a deep, familiar chuckle from the doorway.

I hadn't realized we weren't alone. Roland stood there, his shoulder leaning against the wooden frame, legs crossed, and his hands in the pockets of his jeans. He was so at home here. Our eyes met for the flash of a moment. I looked away, suddenly aware of how hard a heart could pump. How it could boom like a drum, throbbing almost painfully.

"Goodnight," Nan said, patting my arm in the same affectionate way she had touched Roland earlier. Tenderness for her rushed through me. She then patted Roland's cheek before sliding out of the room and down the steps, leaving us alone.

I swallowed. We had spent so much time together over the past ten years, just the two of us, that I couldn't understand why I would now suddenly be so acutely aware of him. Averting my gaze, I mimicked Nan and glanced around the room.

"I love this," I smiled, biting my lip. The silence was too much. "And them."

"I knew you would," Roland's gentle timbre rolled over me, at once putting me at ease and making my gut tighten. A distant drift of memory from high school came to mind—a teacher had told us that the Greeks believed all emotion was in the stomach, in the butterflies, and the gut feelings. I remembered thinking it was foolish, stupid even—but I understood it now.

My hands were shaking and I crossed my arms, as though it could settle the confusing rush of nerves running through my veins.

"Where—"

"Well—"

We both spoke at the same time and broke off. Roland smiled and ran a hand through his hair. I tore my eyes away, remembering how it had felt to touch his hair, how soft it had been. Warmth flooded my cheeks and I looked at my backpack on the chair. Roland moved for it before I could and placed it on the bed. The gesture was kind—but my heart did terrible things to me. It made me so acutely aware of him and I pushed back against it.

Suddenly, it felt as though every inch of me, every thought was focused solely upon him. Was that even possible?

I had been close to him like this before. At parties, or weddings when we danced together. He'd held me in his arms, so why now did he seem to take up this entire room?

Swallowing, I murmured my thanks, refusing to meet his gaze. "Where's the bathroom?" I asked, finishing my earlier question.

"First door on the left, at the top of the stairs."

I nodded, it was my turn to run my fingers through my hair, a nervous gesture. I flipped it over my shoulder. "Do you want to go first, or I can wait to shower, if you need to shower, or do, or just, yeah…" I broke off, flummoxed and hating myself. It was like the statue room all over again. The thought of a shower had made me nervous like a teenager. Oh, how I hoped someday I would grow up and be an adult.

"You can go first. I'll probably shower in the morning."

I nodded, holding tight to what little sanity I seemed to have left, I found my bathroom bag and turned back to him. He'd moved silently back toward the doorway, giving me space, his hand resting on the knob. "Goodnight, Dani," he smiled and his eyes crinkled in the same way I'd seen his Pap's.

He walked past the stairs and without a backward glance entered the room that mirrored mine. Later that night, it took more concentration and effort than I thought to fall asleep.

CHAPTER 18

Roland had never been the kind of man to sleep in. For years he'd told me that sleeping in wasted away too much of the day, that sunrises were like the drawing back of a curtain to reveal the first act of an exciting adventure. No matter how he'd spun the essence of the morning to me, I'd never really believed him.

But it seemed here in Scotland my nerves wouldn't let me sleep in too long. For the first time in my life, I was ready to see what early morning had to offer and I didn't want to waste away in bed—even though the mountain of blankets was heavy enough to tempt me.

I'd rushed to get ready, throwing on a pair of jeans, a simple long-sleeve shirt, and ran a brush through my hair. Quietly, I slipped down the stairs, only making more noise when I heard the gentle murmur of voices, and smelled the coffee wafting from the kitchen.

"Ahh, good morning, Dani," Pap said, walking by with a mug in hand and glasses dipping off the end of his nose. He peered at me over the tops of them. "Can I tempt you with a cup of coffee?"

"Yes, please," I bit my lip debating, "actually can I have it in a bit. I was thinking of going down to the beach. Is Roland in the living room?" I hooked my thumb over my shoulder and Pap chuckled.

"No, and he won't be up for at least another hour."

Odd. I'd never heard of Roland sleeping in past six. I wondered what it was about this place that changed so many things about him. Perhaps, here, on what felt like the other side of the world, we had switched places.

"Oh," was all I said and glanced out one of the windows. I thought I could see the glimmer of disgruntled waves churning in the distance. "I may still go take a look. Can you let him know where I've gone?"

"Of course, but take some coffee with you."

A moment later I was bundled up in my coat, a coffee thermos in hand and the wind whipping my hair in every which direction. I wished I had thought to grab a hairband. Stuffing it down my coat would have to do.

My boots crunched into the near-frozen sand making an odd whistling sound with each step, but I didn't mind as my eyes rested on the water. Here the beach was tucked between rocky outcroppings and surrounded by tall grasses that bowed to the wind. The waves were gentler, more at peace than other beaches I'd been to. The waters lapping against the sand with almost halfhearted attempts. For some reason it made me smile.

I had the distinct feeling that everything moved slower here—as though more in harmony with the way the natural world shifted. Perhaps it was why I felt the release of stress, of burden. I hadn't even thought of work yet, or what the day would bring.

For the first time in a long time, I was simply at peace with the day. Why had I ever struggled so hard against it?

Sipping on the coffee, I let it warm my insides as I trudged closer to the edge of the water and stared out toward the horizon. To either side of me was a jagged shore. Far off to the right, the land jutted toward the ocean—a near-purple shadow, while to the left, in the distance, I could spot a few white-washed buildings. I wondered if that was the small town we had passed through last night.

Thinking of our adventures in that car, I laughed. I might need to wash my mouth out with soap. My mom certainly would have if she'd heard what I said. As though in memory, I ran a finger over my lips and smiled. Perhaps saltwater could purge those words.

Passing an outcropping of rocks, I carefully kept my boots from getting wet. The rocks were sharp and freezing beneath my fingers, but what met me on the other side was breathtaking. A beach stretched for what seemed to be a mile, though I was no great judge of distance. Gnarled rocks crested high above my head and I wondered what the view must be like from the swaying grass peeking over the edge.

How long I stayed on the beach, I wasn't sure, but it was long enough to walk from one end to the other, and for my coffee to have grown lukewarm. Being here in this place, I realized my statement to Roland the night before had been more than true. In some ways, I felt my heart belonged here in Scotland.

I was nearly back to where I had started when I saw Roland wave from down the beach. I smiled and waved back. The sunlight shimmering off the water helped to ease the chill of the wind stinging my nose.

"Pap sent me to find out if you had been taken away with the tide," Roland's voice carried on the wind as he came closer.

I laughed, dispelling his words. "Not yet."

His grin matched my own as he reached me. "Good morning," he said, a little breathless and smiling. My stomach flipped.

If I had thought Roland was handsome in the moonlight, it was nothing compared to how he looked now. His hair, always so dark, seemed to shimmer with streaks of near auburn when reflecting the sun. That smile I had come to notice more and more was now growing as he took in the view I had just been staring at, but it was when he turned to look back down at me that I inhaled sharply. Those eyes.

I could get lost in those eyes.

Perhaps it was why I had always shied away from recognizing what was there—or at least what I thought was there. His eyes reminded me of the loch last night. Dark, mysterious, but filled with enticing secrets that I knew, if explored, could drown me.

Fighting back my reaction, I forced myself to stand on firm ground and push my wild hair away from my face. I could only imagine how I must look.

"Good morning," I said softly, almost uncertain.

His smile grew. "Have you explored enough for the day?"

"Not at all."

"Good."

"Why's that?"

"Because we're going to town."

"We are?"

"Yes," he confirmed and then turned back in the direction he had come with a cock of his head in beckoning. "Come on."

I nodded, fighting back a smile, and followed him back to the house. In the early morning light, his grandparent's home was taller than I remembered and yet simpler. Small cracks in the stone, shabby patches where the ocean wind had worn down all that was rough, but my original thoughts still stood the test of morning—it was quaint and all things pleasant.

Perhaps it was my nature to view things in such a way. My mother had once told me that she admired the way I could always see the beauty in a place or a person. I don't know if that was entirely true, but I tried to see things that way. I think after a time it just became a habit.

A lot of times the very things that seemed abnormal were what made a place or person beautiful. Who would want to live in a world where everything was utterly perfect—everything the same? I liked the unexpected beauty of chipped cups or broken barn doors because such things told a story. Just like scars, those seen and unseen told stories of character and strength.

Nan bustled around the kitchen scratching a list on a piece of paper to give to Roland, her voice filling the space. My mind drifted as she walked and I found myself drawn to the fire in the hearth of the living room. Holding my hands out over the warmth, I waited for some feeling to come back into the tips.

On the mantle were some pictures I hadn't seen up close. There was one of Nan and Pap standing in front of the Eiffel Tower that appeared to be taken in the '80s according to the shoulder pads and high-waisted jeans. And then there were a few with Roland at varying ages. I looked at each in turn, my eyes settling on one of him between his grandparents, his arms wrapped around their shoulders, and his grin bright and jovial with wild abandon. I'd never seen him look so free. It made me smile involuntarily by just looking at it.

"He looks just like him, doesn't he?"

I hadn't heard Pap come into the room. Glancing over my shoulder I didn't understand his question until I looked back at the picture again. This picture was in France too, standing before the front gates of the Palace of Versailles, but the style of clothes was all wrong. Staring at the picture now I realized Roland's hair was longer, and yet…it didn't make sense. And the photo itself, it was a little faded…and I wasn't sure if Roland had ever been to France.

Then it clicked.

This wasn't Roland. This was his father.

I hoped my mouth wasn't hanging open as I stared. In all the years I'd known Roland he'd never mentioned his dad, had never brought him up. I had just assumed he didn't know who he was.

"This is your son?" I asked almost needing confirmation, even though it was obvious. Questions were flying rapidly through my mind.

Pap smiled, a vague ghost of the one his son wore in the picture. "He was a good man."

Was. That one word confirmed what I'd feared all along.

Roland's father had died.

"Dani, you ready?"

I blinked quickly, as though to dispel the lump that had suddenly formed in my throat. It didn't work. "Coming."

Pap patted my arm and I wondered if he knew that his grandson never mentioned his father. I wanted to stay and ask about this man—this mysterious person who I hadn't even known existed. And somehow it stung.

There was betrayal, or at least, pieces of it. I'd shared so much of myself with Roland over the years, but he'd never shared this part of him.

Leaving the cottage, the sun was all bright and warm—and when Roland turned back toward the beach, leaving the car behind, I followed without hesitation. It seemed we would be walking to town—and I thanked my lucky stars to be in the open air. I didn't know if I could handle a car ride with him right now, sitting so close, knowing what I now knew. Or rather, didn't know.

"This place is surreal isn't it?" Roland broke into my swirling thoughts, his thumbs hooked through the straps of the empty backpack we would use to carry all the items Nan had asked us to purchase.

"It is." I sighed, enjoying the view from the high rocky sides of the beach, the sands far below us, and the water glinting. "All of this has been surreal."

"Scotland can be that way."

"Not just Scotland, all of it."

He peered at me. "What do you mean?"

"When else are we going to get a chance like this? I mean, what were the chances of running into each other at the airport?" It seemed like a lifetime ago.

"Not very high," he laughed, his mood lighter than my own. I couldn't seem to pull that picture out of my mind, and I hated that it affected me so acutely.

"Exactly," I agreed. "How many times have you visited Gairloch?"

"Ahh, probably over ten times, I mean it's been almost every summer since they moved here, what, let's see, eleven years ago. So yeah, probably ten times in the summer and a handful of visits here and there, so maybe actually sixteen or seventeen in the last eleven years. It somehow seems like more since I usually stay for so long."

"How long are you going to stay this time?"

"That sort of depends," he said, his voice growing softer.

I continued to watch my feet, concentrating on not stumbling over stones. "On what?"

"Well, I wouldn't mind staying for a bit since we just got here, but I know you need to get back."

Something inside me warmed. He wanted to be here with me, to share this adventure, and he wanted to fly home together. I pushed the meaning behind all of that aside.

"Okay," was all I said.

"Were you thinking of leaving so soon?"

"No, I mean, I don't know." The wind pulled some of my hair free from my jacket. I'd forgotten to grab a hairband again. "I'll have to put in some hours of serious work soon, but I think I could stay a week."

Even though he didn't look at me, I saw the corner of his mouth lift. Though many things between us were confusing to me right now, this never would be. If there was one thing I had always loved, it was making Roland smile. It never ceased to make me grin in return.

He deserved the world and so many didn't realize that about him. They didn't know how often he smiled or laughed but it was never to the fullest extent. He reserved those laughs and smiles for only the purest and most joyful moments.

I didn't know what the future held, but I did know that there were pieces of me that wished to always be the one to draw those kinds of smiles from him. Thinking of that picture of his dad again, I could see it now—the perfect resemblance in a carefree smile.

Roland was a perfect reflection, nearly a twin to his father. Those genes ran strong, so why didn't he ever talk of him?

As we reached the outer buildings of the charming town of Gairloch, I decided to put it all behind me. Maybe someday Roland would tell me in his own time.

Roland showed me all around town, or what there was of it. We walked and talked, popping into this shop, that bakery, and little stores all along the road. I loved every bit of it and could see how his grandparents had decided to settle here. Roland even pointed out a little café that from the window appeared to house cozy booths and when the door opened, I got a whiff of the coffee brewing inside.

Yes, this would be a great place to work. I told Roland as much and mentally made a note to return there the following day. From what I understood, Roland and his Pap were planning to go fishing—something they often did.

With all of the items Nan had written down on the piece of paper crossed off and loaded into the now full backpack, we began our return trek. We walked mostly in silence, every now and then commenting on some small observation, or bringing up a memory. It was our usual way, and yet, it didn't sit right.

Perhaps it was this new knowledge—this insight into a piece of Roland that he had never shared with me. As we walked my frustration slightly turned to anger. How many times had he pushed me to reveal my secrets, to bare my soul? And yet, he hadn't shared in kind.

The more I thought about it, the more frustrated I became. Especially when thinking of the time I had told him of the difficulties of having a father who was deaf—and how guilty I felt for even saying those words. Of course, I could speak to my father, but there were little things I wanted or felt I had missed out on. For instance, I'd never overheard my parents saying, "I love you." Or how I'd never fallen asleep in a car listening to them talk. I'd told Roland as much in high school and he'd listened to me, but he'd never shared about his father.

"Why didn't you tell me about him?" I blurted; my frustration having risen to a level that should have told me to turn my thoughts elsewhere.

Perhaps it was the tone of my voice, but Roland stopped his brow furrowing. Behind him, the waves continued to flicker and shimmer in the midday, winter sun.

"Who?"

"Your father." There, I had said it. The word that we had always avoided when it came to his life now stood between us.

"No," he shook his head immediately, "we're not going to talk about him."

"Why not?"

"Because I said so."

"Oh, so you don't like it when I push to know more about you?" I was growing angrier by the second and I didn't entirely know why—perhaps it was out of the hurt. "You always ask me about my feelings, my family, my childhood, but I'm, not allowed to ask about yours?"

"No, you're not." He said the words point-blank, finally meeting my gaze. I nearly flinched when I saw the anger there. He wouldn't budge.

"I thought you didn't even know who your dad was." There was hurt in my voice, I wondered if Roland heard it too.

A muscle tightened in his jaw. "What did Pap tell you?"

I blinked quickly at the ice in his voice. I'd been wrong to tread down this path. Pain lingered here. "Nothing…never mind, just forget it." We stared at one another.

Roland sighed and ran his fingers through his hair.

"Did he tell you how he died? Fine, I will give you the facts." He shrugged as though it was nothing to him, but his eyes said differently. "He was a great dad, actually, but he felt like he'd given up on his dreams of seeing the world too young. He couldn't be kept in an office, so he drank. And when that didn't satisfy, he left. According to the note, it was to spare my mom and me. I was seven when I read that note. A year later my mom received a call from Pap. My dad had gone swimming at a party while drunk. No one realized he'd drowned until the next morning."

All the color drained from my face and I stared up at him as all the beauty of the world around us seemed to fade. Tears pooled in my eyes as I realized so many things about Roland that now made sense.

Roland had never had a drink. He was so practical, always swearing that hard work was the way to get what you wanted. His loyalty was unmatched, and he never shirked responsibilities. All of it, defined by his father's failures.

"And that," he pointed toward my face, "is exactly why I didn't tell anyone in Landing about him. That pity, right there. After a while, you get tired of seeing it."

My face heated and I looked away before the tears could escape. How could I have been so stupid? I had thought him selfish to hold back these pieces of himself, but I was the selfish one. Selfish enough to think that our friendship was false because he didn't fully trust me with his past. So self-centered and careless.

"I'm sorry," I said, and quickly added, "not just for what happened, but for pushing you. I won't bring it up again."

Without another word, I began to walk forward. I heard him sigh behind me. Before too long his boots began to crunch through the grass in my wake.

"You would have liked him," he said with forced casualness. I kept walking but nodded so he would know I heard. "He had one of the best laughs, but that's really the only thing I remember. The rest of my memories are pieces of what I've been told."

That made sense—only the most distinct memories stuck.

"But I remember when Mom told me he was gone."

Something inside me broke at the thought of young Roland having to go through this pain. The world could be so cruel.

I stopped, turning around to look at him. "You don't have to tell me any of this."

He closed the remaining steps between us, towering above me. His eyes roved over me, the edges of them strained. Uncertainty hovered. We stared at one another for a time, his fathomless eyes searching mine. For a moment, his breath caught and he blinked.

"I know I don't have to, but I think I want to."

I reached for his hand and squeezed it, hoping it would help him to continue.

"He left and died on the same date. August 9th."

"Oh," I said, something clicking in the back of my mind, a far-off memory.

"Yeah, not my favorite day. I guess that's one lie I have to come clean on."

I nodded. *August 9th*.

For years he'd told me August 9th was an important day, one he liked to spend alone with his mother. Our group of friends had pushed him about it once, to the point of teasing that nearly went too far—he'd then said it was his mother's birthday. I'd known he was lying then, had known it because he'd told me his mother's real birthday was in January. But I hadn't pushed then, and I was sorry I had now.

How had I not realized that he'd always trusted me with this secret all along? He'd not given me the reason, but he'd stared at me that night so many years ago when our friends teased him—I'd met his gaze and he'd known I knew. And I had simply nodded.

He'd ducked his chin slightly in relief, a silent thank you.

Squeezing his hand again, I let my fingers fall away and turned to leave when he reached for my arm, holding me there. He blinked and then looked away. His thumb ran down my jacket to my exposed wrist, across my palm and back again—shooting little currents of fire up my arm. It was as though his fingers touched my heart.

"Dani, I—can I—I need to ask you something."

My heart pinched painfully. "Yes?"

His voice was softer than I had ever heard it before—so gentle, almost like a caress. "Do you remember that night we spent on the trampoline, at the bonfire?"

I nodded, my mouth going dry.

"Well, now that I've told you those things, I need to tell you about that night—" he broke off, his thumb tracing my wrist again, his eyes blinking, looking down, before meeting my own once more. He was struggling with the words.

"That was before we all left for school, it was August…" my voice trailed off and I realized what I had been missing. "Oh, Roland. Oh." My other hand covered my mouth as I uttered the words. "You were grieving your father and all we were doing was celebrating."

Roland's brow furrowed and he blinked as though confused.

"We were all so blind." I thought of the tear I had seen escape his eye and it nearly broke my heart. Was this the mystery behind that tear? It was far more painful than I had thought. "I'm sorry, Roland," I said and leaned in to hug him. "So very sorry, we should have realized. I should have realized."

His arms hesitated before he wrapped them around me, holding me tight against his chest. I wondered how it was he switched the control so easily. I was supposed to be comforting him, but he seemed to be comforting me.

A soft smile turned the corners of my lips. This was how it was supposed to be, wasn't it? Friends, supporting one another.

"Should we go back now?" I murmured, not wanting to let him go.

"Probably," he said, and slowly, oh so slowly, his arms slipped from around my shoulders.

Smiling up at him, I asked, "Am I forgiven then?"

He chuckled. "You never had anything to be forgiven for, at least not with me."

"But we just established my complete idiocy as to what you were going through that night."

He stared down at our feet and when he looked up again a mournful smile raised the corners of his mouth. "You and I remember things very differently."

My brow furrowed and I wanted to ask him what he meant. Somehow, someway I realized he was putting me off again. Whatever ground I had thought I gained in understanding was suddenly lost.

Roland grabbed my hand and pulled me along behind him, leading the way back to the house. Every now and then he would squeeze my fingers gently—he might as well have been squeezing my heart.

CHAPTER 19

Danielle,

Everything looks wonderful. We are so pleased with how this has turned
out. I agree with you, I think the color palette was a bit too bold, I
like the second option the most. Thank you for all of your insights, and
please enjoy the rest of your break in Scotland. I'm so glad you enjoyed
Chatsworth, it was one of my favorite places.
We will chat when you are back in your office.
Cheers,
Kendra

The email from Mrs. Kent warmed my insides as much as the coffee mug that
rested between my hands. After a slow morning and hearty breakfast with Nan, I'd
walked to town to catch up on some of the work that had been urgently waiting for
me.

Hours had slipped by and I was thankful Nan had stuffed me to the gills with what
she called a traditional Scottish breakfast. I didn't know what to think of the black
pudding, but the beans were quite good—even if it was the earliest I had ever eaten
beans in my life.

I was just beginning to feel the weight of unfinished tasks slip away when Mrs.
Kent's email had appeared. Finally, we both seemed happy with the look of her
website. Now that I had the vision board and outline in production, it wouldn't take
me more than a day or two to build the rest of the site. The other minute features and
details could be added later.

"Another for ya'?" the barista asked, his Scottish brogue so thick it seemed to
belong to a man much older than his adolescent face.

"I'm fine, thanks." I smiled, not wanting to overdo the caffeine intake. I'd had plenty and with afternoon creeping ever closer I would be hard-pressed to fall asleep if I drank any more coffee.

"Nothin' to eat?"

I shook my head and thanked the boy who had checked on me every hour or so. The delightful clink of spoons stirring cream and sugar along with the subtle murmur of conversations all around helped to still the unease of what had passed between me and Roland the day before.

Every time I thought about it, my heart seemed to stutter and my hands grew sweaty. I wasn't sure if it was fear or excitement, or a mix of both. All I knew is that part of me wanted to cry and the other part wanted to laugh. I'd found the cure was to simply concentrate on my computer and put all thoughts of Roland out of my mind.

Scotland was becoming a land that messed with everything I thought I knew.

Tossing that thought aside, I continued to outline the design for Mrs. Kent's website. After a few minutes, I was pleased to realize that I could control the direction of my thoughts, and therefore, I would be able to control my feelings. And that was exactly what needed to be done.

I didn't know what to feel when it came to Roland right now, and I didn't want to contemplate it. We were friends, and I refused to think there was something more going on. Because to even wonder would jeopardize our friendship, and I couldn't do that. I wouldn't do that—because to lose his friendship would be something I couldn't even fully comprehend.

A ping signaled a message in the top right corner of my computer. I blinked at the name.

Mason.

Ignoring the familiar jolt that tended to flip my heart where his name was concerned, I clicked on the window and read through his message twice before letting it settle.

> Hey. I know you're out of town, your mom said something about Scotland. If you get a chance, can you call me? Need some advice.

And just like that, the bubble that I had been living in, popped. Pieces of myself had been left in Landing, pieces I didn't want to completely deal with. It had been easier to just set all of it aside—to ignore it as though it didn't matter. And I had done just that—I'd run away from it all.

But here Mason was. Mason, the boy, now man, who'd caught my eye in middle school. Oh, I was a fool.

What would Charlotte do? I wondered and then flinched away from that thought. She was far from an inspiration—or even a character to model my life after. She'd ended up with only a parlor to keep her happy, had signed away her soul for something to call her own—but the cost was so high in Mr. Collins.

Biting my lip, I hastened to write back to Mason. Perhaps I had caught him at a time when he was free. Taking a deep breath, I forced myself to be as casual as possible, even as my heart thudded loudly in my ears.

> Hey! I won't be able to call…but I can text. Currently in a coffee shop knocking out some work.

I bit my thumbnail, waiting, and glanced around. All ease of mind had fled, and what had once seemed such a cozy atmosphere faded out of focus. I tried to concentrate on designing something when the ping went off again.

> *You never stop working huh?*

Then the three dots appeared. I waited impatiently for him to finish typing—my leg bouncing.

> *I need some advice, and you've always been good with this stuff.*

> Okay...I'll see what I can do.

I had a sudden inkling of where this conversation was going and I wanted to pull back, to tell him I was busy. But it wasn't his fault that I had helped

132

him in the past—and I did value our relationship—friendship, whatever this thing was called.

I watched the three dots blink over and over again, for what seemed like an eternity. Finally, his message appeared.

> *Nancy and I got into an argument last night. She expected me to propose. She said I had given her the wrong idea by having her move here. She expected us to get engaged, but I think it's too soon. I want to live together for a while and see if that works, ya know? I don't want to rush things like I did with Ellen. I need to know that this is it. I like Nancy…love her. But I don't think we're ready for marriage. Any advice…???*

I stared at the words, looking at them from multiple angles. To me, it seemed more obvious that what had been done had happened in the wrong order. But I was different than many people my age.

Suddenly I realized how different I was from Mason. Had we always been that way? Our priorities so skewed? Remembering what Roland had said about Mason and his goals, I began to realize it was all true. Mason was a good guy, but wasn't he always out for Mason? When was the last time Mason had asked me about my life, or anyone else for that matter?

I sighed and began to type, not sure if I had the right words to offer him or even advice. More than anything, I knew I didn't want to give it—that I didn't like how even seeing his name burst the bubble of calm I had carefully concocted after leaving Landing. Or the fact that I even had an emotional response to him at all.

> **Had you guys talked about marriage before she moved?**

> *Yes. But nothing official.*

I rolled my eyes. My guess was it had seemed like a very official conversation to Nancy. Thinking back to Kari's wedding, I remembered watching this woman catch the bouquet, and then the looks she had given Mason while dancing were anything but subtle.

No, there was no way this woman had thought a conversation about marriage was anything but official—anything but certain.

Knowing Mason as I did, he tended to avoid anything that made him feel the least bit uncomfortable. It was either that or he was just very unaware of those who didn't immediately affect him. In his mind, his plans were set and he would be the one to determine if anything needed to change. It was a strength and a weakness of his. A strength in that he was so sure of himself—a weakness because he didn't foresee that anyone could think differently than him. It wasn't that he pushed his ideas on others, he simply followed a logical pattern to a conclusion and couldn't understand how anyone could ever come up with a different answer.

Where did you leave it?

Leave what?

The conversation.

Oh. She left.

I blinked at that in surprise.

She left Landing?

No. Stayed with Kari. They've become friends.

Of course, they had. I tried not to feel the bit of betrayal at this revelation about Kari. But it didn't hurt as much as it should have. Kari and I had been drifting apart for years—even before her wedding. I had been her maid of honor more out of childhood promises than anything else.

We'd drifted down different paths since high school. And it was more than that. She never could understand me, how deeply I felt, or how I longed for something deeper than surface level. In fact, Roland was one of the few who knew I longed for more than the status quo.

You need to talk to her. Tell her how you feel. Did you say that you felt it was too soon?

No. I didn't get a chance. She stormed out before I could say anything. Am I wrong here? We've only been dating for 6 months…???

I paused; my fingers poised over the keys. What could I say to all of this? This wasn't the first time I'd given Mason advice in his relationships. Nancy wasn't the first woman to have stormed out on him. I wondered if that had more to say about Mason or these women.

In some ways, it seemed like the women who caused the most drama got the most attention. Kari and I had always wondered about that in school. We'd joked that maybe if we cried openly in the cafeteria, we would be able to get a boyfriend.

Kari had dared me once to try and cry in front of Mason. That was one of those memories I preferred to leave completely covered. I'd worked up some tears and cried, sitting in the bed of his truck, making up some story about how my heart was broken.

The result had been Mason giving me an awkward pat on the shoulder and asking if I wanted something to drink. He'd handed me his water bottle and then called Kari over to comfort me.

Even now, nearly twelve years later, I still blushed at what I had done. I returned to the conversation at hand, forcing back the second-hand embarrassment from my younger self.

Idk. But she did move to Landing. That says something about her intentions.

I guess.

Go talk to her. Explain what the holdup is.

Okay…I'll try.

The little dots told me he was saying something more. Then they disappeared, he'd stopped typing. They reappeared again and I waited with bated breath.

Why was I like this? Somehow, from across an ocean, I was still holding out for him. It was moments like these when I disliked who I had become—so desperate, clinging onto false hopes.

Those little dots flashed and I wondered if he would ask about me, about my trip. Only now did I realize he hadn't asked a single question about how I was doing. Maybe, somehow, if I kept this conversation going, he would. Maybe he was trying to figure out what to ask me first.

I watched those little dots, biting my lip. I glanced around, wondering how everyone else seemed completely at ease with the world.

What should I say to her?

Hope burst.

I blinked at the words and half-laughed. Why did I ever think things would change?

Mason was always about Mason. Perhaps, a little unknowingly, but our friendship was always surrounded by his life and his decisions. Did he even know anything about me? Had he ever for one second realized I wanted him?

Various words that I now knew I could say in a blind furry while driving came to mind. As much as I wanted to put them in writing, I knew I never would. Instead, I began to type, the message waiting for me to hit send.

The door to the coffee shop tinkled and for some reason, I looked up. And just like that the clouds slightly parted. Roland scanned the room, his hands fidgeting as he looked for me. I waited until his eyes settled on my table.

His smile could brighten the cloudiest of days.

I grinned back.

He crossed the room in long strides. My heart skipped a beat when he placed one hand on my table and leaned closer to me, his eyes nearly at my level. "Are you done for today? I have a surprise."

Nodding, I hurriedly slipped my things into my bag. With one last glance, I pressed send on the message to Mason, before closing my laptop and following Roland.

For one second I wondered what Mason would make of my message. They were simple words, but ones of freedom, unbinding my heart from whatever hold he had on me.

You'll have to figure that out for yourself.

I'd typed the words with confidence, and by now he'd read them. My phone buzzed in my pocket, but instead of looking, I clicked it to silent mode and followed Roland out the door.

I was in Scotland, with a surprise on the horizon, and no one, not even Mason, could ruin today.

CHAPTER 20

Horses, that was the surprise.

I stared at the black beauty before me. He was nothing like Beardsley who had been all stately and unenthusiastic.

"What's his name?" I asked Roland, nearly breathless. I felt like a child barely containing my excitement.

"Rocon." Roland said the horse's name with a Scottish roll of his tongue, pronouncing it like "Rrr-o-cone." I loved it.

Biting my lip, I stepped forward and patted Rocon's side. He shifted beneath my hand, his shoulder twitching with unspent energy. Anticipation built within me.

Roland helped me into the saddle, lifting me with ease. At least he couldn't see how wide my eyes were as I awkwardly threw my leg over the saddle.

"Are you ready?" Roland asked, his smile growing as he was now seated on his brown horse, the reins resting in his hands.

I nodded quickly.

"I was actually talking to Rocon?" He rolled the 'r' again.

"Were you now, Rrrroland?" I replied with the best Scottish accent I could muster. The surprise in his eyes was worth it, and when he laughed, I smiled and nudged Rocon forward. We picked our way across the sand and gently through the winter wind that whipped all around us.

This time I had remembered to pull my hair back into a French braid, a few loose strands tickled my cheeks. The waves were choppy, their white caps crashing and thrashing as though in a never-ending struggle against the wind.

I loved everything about it, the wind, the sand, the storm clouds on the horizon, the sharp sting of winter air in my nostrils, the thrill of the open beach, and the creaking of the saddle beneath me. The sand seemed so far below, and as we passed by the outcropping of rocks along the beach, the great stretch of open shore met us. I inhaled deeply, the tide was out, the beach wider than before—a mile of possibilities waiting to be taken.

In certain places the water rested in long puddles, stranded from the rest of the ocean.

"I love this!" I exhaled loudly, and put my hands out wide, as though embracing the wind.

Roland laughed, the deep timbre of his voice stirring something within me. "Then let's get going."

His horse danced to the side, slightly agitated. Rocon shifted beneath me, his hooves kicking up loose sand.

"Where?"

"Does it matter?" he challenged. I had never seen this side of Roland. So carefree, so completely at home—it warmed my heart.

Laughing I nodded, "Onward?"

A gleam entered Roland's eyes and I couldn't help but notice how handsome he looked astride a horse. This stirring thing between us was completely new and confusing, but the picture he made captured all of my attention. There he sat, one gloved hand on his leg, the other grasping the reins. His broad shoulders were casually straightened, his muscular legs bracing the saddle. He was all things masculine and robust. A sudden gale lifted his hair, stirring it in a wave that matched the tumultuous feelings colliding within me.

He turned to me then, one side of his mouth quirking in a wry grin, at once playful and serious. "You told me you always wanted to give a horse its head, to know what it would feel like to ride at full speed."

A thrill of excitement ran through my veins. He'd listened to me—and he'd heard not just the want but the longing.

I inhaled, only this time it was due to the thrill of excitement running through my veins. He'd truly listened.

I stared at the open beach and took in the gift Roland had given me. A childhood longing, about to be fulfilled. My heart fluttered in anticipation.

"I'm guessing this is going to be a little more intense than the galloping I did as a kid?" My voice wavered only slightly.

Excitement was radiating off Roland and the horses seemed to catch it too, both of them shifting, waiting, prancing. I steadied my breath and prepared my muscles for what was to come. Muscles had memory and I was counting on them to remember.

I laughed nervously and grasped the reins all the tighter. Beside me, Roland sat straighter and when I caught his eye, I spotted a gleam of some adventurous side of him that I'd never seen before. With a quick wink, he beamed at me, his hand slapping Rocon's rump. That was all it took.

Rocon shot forward.

Nothing could have prepared me for the sheer power and exhilaration of the horse beneath me. I'd ridden fast before, but nothing like this.

I was at once in control and not at all—leaning forward, my seat light as Rocon thundered beneath me. I was flying—the waves of the ocean crashing, the wind pulling at me as the powerful muscles of the black beast extended and contracted. As though from far off I heard the thudding of hooves and knew Roland was following.

Life became a taught wire of thrill—danger and carelessness colliding. It was living.

We reached the end of the beach and Rocon slowed beneath me, his hooves sliding gently in the sand. He snorted heavily and when I turned him back the way we had come, I couldn't believe we had crossed the entire space in so short a time. I viewed the beach like an open road stretching before us. Rocon sidled in the sand and I knew he wanted to go again.

Breathless, I met Roland's gaze, his excitement matching my own. I knew my eyes were wide from the adrenaline pumping through my veins— from the soaring in my heart. Seeing his wind-blown hair got me thinking of my own. For some reason, I needed to feel the wind through every part of me.

I wanted to leave all fear behind, to let go. I'd set Mason behind me, I'd finally opened my hands of him. Breathing came easier as I realized the enormity of what had happened in my heart. Reaching up, I fumbled with my braid, shaking it out until my hair was tugging in the wind. I laughed then, facing the ocean and loving this feeling of unbridled liberty.

Roland was watching me when I turned back to him, his eyes brimming with joy and something else I didn't want to name. When his gaze softened, tension pulled between us. I met it head-on. Winking at him and cocking my chin toward the open shore before us.

"Again?" I challenged. It was then that I remembered what Roland had said at the airport. He liked to ride, and he liked to ride fast.

In unison, we kicked our horses into a full-throttled sprint. All was storm and wind and power. All of it colliding for attention, all of it grasping at me, but it was too late because I was coursing faster than the wind.

I laughed, and tears of joy reached my eyes, stinging my cheeks as we raced back the way we had come. Beside me, I heard Roland hoot and when I saw him, leaning over his horse, his arms bobbing in rhythm, his hair whipped tightly against his head and his jacket humped in the wind, I laughed again.

In that instant, I knew we were living a near dream. A moment I would come back to in days to come. This was to be a memory that I would forever treasure in my heart.

Roland's eyes met mine and the emotion there was nearly overpowering, its essence wrapped in pure hope, joy, and that lingering nameless passion. With a wild cry like I had never heard before, he whooped and urged his horse to run with even greater speed—he did like to ride fast. Running straight through a puddle left behind from the tide, saltwater kicked up onto my face and skin, tangled into my hair, and I reveled in it.

It was reckless abandon, and I never wanted it to end.

Back and forth we crossed the beach, time lost for a moment until we eventually dismounted to give the horses a break. The ocean roared, even more disgruntled than when we had begun—a storm lingered on the horizon.

"Thank you," I sighed.

We had been silent for a while, sitting in the sand, our shoulders nearly touching. I wondered if my hair looked as crazy as Roland's, all wind-whipped and carefree. I liked it. Seeing him like this was refreshing.

"You don't need to thank me."

"I feel like I do. None of this would have happened without you."

"Ah," he waved a hand in dismissal, "you were already here, I just had to give you a nudge in the right direction," he bumped my shoulder for emphasis.

I don't think he fully understood how bleak my trip to the UK had been before he turned up. There had been nothing healing about this journey until he came along. I wondered about that—parts of me wanting to lean closer to him, while the other, stronger part threw up warnings. We were friends, just friends.

Friendship. I would focus on that word. It was our safe place.

Straightening, I stood and brushed the sand from the backs of my legs. Having some distance from him was helpful—I could think a little more clearly when I wasn't so aware of the warmth that seemed to radiate from his body.

Patting Rocon on the neck, I leaned into him, breathing in the salt and sweat clinging to his sides. With an idle hand, I played with his mane, smiling when his large eye moved to look at me.

"Hi," I whispered. He made no intention of having heard me and that was quite all right. "Roland?"

"Hmm?"

"How do you ever leave this place?" I was staring out over the ocean now, loving the way the water churned and furled. It was all so beautiful, even if it was cold—so very cold.

"I don't know." I heard him get to his feet. "It's never easy to leave, especially leaving Nan and Pap behind, but it makes me appreciate the time I get to spend with them. I don't take it for granted." By the end of his words, he was standing not far behind me.

I swallowed. I needed the distance between us, this was all too new. Retreating slightly to the side, I found the rock wall that ran along the beach. It had been our shelter from the wind.

Pushing back on my tangled hair, I could feel Roland watching me. "It sounds like you're quite the romantic." I teased, finally meeting his gaze.

I don't know what I had expected to see, but the look in his eyes was coming unfurled again. There was no denying what was there, I could see it as plain as the waves rolling behind him. It was that unnamed emotion—that curious power that lingered in the depths of his dark eyes. I couldn't let myself recognize it fully. I wasn't ready.

Friendship. I clung to the word again. I would keep this on the proper boundary lines, I had to. Everything could be at stake and I hadn't had time to think about if I even wanted it to be. Did I care for Roland in that way? Could I?

It was all too much and yet not enough. I was at war within myself.

A question was coming, I could sense it. When he didn't speak, I met his eyes once more. A mistake—for the question was there, lingering in the depths of his warm gaze.

He stepped closer and I pressed into the rocks at my back, my hands tucked near my sides. Blinking quickly, I wanted to look away, but couldn't. He stared down at me, our gazes holding, searching. I felt helpless.

At the last moment, he shifted to lean his back against the wall, clearing my view. Seeing the sky let me breathe once more.

"I haven't done that in ages." Roland sounded as though he was confessing something.

143

"Done what?"

"Ride that fast. Pap used to go with me, but he's not as young as he once was."

I could only imagine what riding like that would do to a man Pap's age. Though he seemed robust, I could already feel which muscles would be sore and aching tomorrow.

Roland glanced down at me, his brow furrowed in curiosity.

"What?" I asked and he shrugged. "No, what?"

"You're very quiet."

"Oh," I didn't know what else to say to that, and at the same time realized it proved his point. "Then tell me something," I challenged.

His mouth quirked slightly, appreciating my candor.

His mouth. I'd made the mistake of looking at his mouth.

Just then a sharp breeze tugged at my hair and whipped thick strands across my face. I hastened to tuck them behind my ear and into the collar of my jacket but a few strands were stuck in my mouth until suddenly they weren't. Roland's fingers brushed against my lips and then my cheek as he pulled the strands from my mouth and tucked them behind my ear.

All breath stilled, holding, then releasing. My chest rose and fell heavily.

He shifted before me then. It was the subtlest of movements—hardly noticeable, but when all I could see was him, and when he rested his hand over my shoulder, it suddenly felt as though we had traveled a mile to stand this close together.

"What should I tell you?" He still hadn't removed his other hand from my cheek. My skin beneath it warmed.

"I don't know," my voice was a hoarse whisper—parts of me clawing at the rock at my back to flee. I couldn't do this, not here.

"How about if I tell you how I've always loved this place, but now, being here with you, sharing all of this with you…" he trailed off and shook his head slightly. I could so easily reach up and pull his mouth to mine. The thought made me blush. "Dani, you brighten this place in ways you can't even understand."

Something inside me hitched and I breathed deeply to maintain control. The wall of our friendship seemed to be crumbling beneath us, but I was too afraid to find out what it all meant.

"You've always been that way, brightening my darkest days. Sometimes you don't even know it, but you do."

Had I not thought the same thing when I'd seen him in the airport? Was this how it was supposed to be—this deep longing for a person who made you enjoy the day, who made you aware of how lucky you were to be alive? Was that all this was?

As though in response, my heart stuttered.

No, there was more here than mere feeling. There was an ache, but whether it was good or bad I didn't know.

Roland's thumb brushed against my cheek in idle circles. It felt right and new, and warm, and confusing all at the same time. In his eyes, there was no longer any restraint. The way he was looking at me now could make me go to pieces all at once—the force of it was more powerful than anything I could have imagined.

His gaze drifted to my lips. My breath caught, and I forced myself to speak. "That's what we do for each other. We pull each other up." I smiled slightly, nervously, very aware that my smile was only drawing more attention to my lips. Roland noticed too. I took a deep breath and pressed on "I never can thank you enough for all of this—for helping me. I was already headed home—but you knew that," I rambled. "Without you, I never would have experienced this. I would have missed out on this adventure."

His thumb that had been gently caressing my cheek while I spoke, stilled. And though he tried to hide it, I saw the wall return to his eyes. It was as though I had slapped him—as though the tether of what was stirring between us had snapped.

I blinked, wondering what I had done, what I had said. I ran over my words again but it didn't make any sense. He'd nearly flinched when I'd said the word 'adventure.' If he hadn't been standing so close, I probably would have missed it, but his breath had nearly mingled with mine. I'd seen the change.

How was he still such a mystery to me?

An ear-splitting crack of thunder blasted across the sky—I yelped in surprise and the horses bolted up the hill and back toward the house. As one, Roland and I looked out over the furious ocean. The clouds were morphing and shifting, each darker than the next.

"Come on," Roland said, snatching up my hand.

A flash of lightning exploded in a forked wire, Roland grabbed me and held me to his chest, my back shoved into the rock wall as the thunder jolted through us with an overpowering rumble.

Of all the things in the world, Roland knew I didn't like storms. Rain and snow didn't bother me, but when it came to lightning and thunder, I never wanted to be outside. It terrified me.

I just needed to get inside—then I would be fine. Roland grasped my hand and together we ran up the hill and back to the cottage. Only once did I stumble when more thunder rolled overhead.

Pap was already securing the horses when Roland sent me inside and left to help his grandfather. Standing in the living room, I took what seemed like the first real breath since Roland had touched my cheek. I didn't know how, and I didn't know why, but something between us had shifted—altered. Forever changed.

Whether for better, or worse, I didn't know.

As though condoning the disappointment and dread that was beginning to course through me, the roar of rain reached my ears and covered the cottage in a blanket of quaking uncertainty.

CHAPTER 21

I hadn't always been afraid of storms. At least that was why I had ventured outside to watch a lightning storm as a child. I was eight and invincible when I stepped out into the puddles, barefooted and soaked to the skin. I'd stared up at the sky, watching the wind bend and shake the trees. There had been no fear in me as I squinted into the bright flashes forking and splitting all that was dark and dangerous.

But when lightning hit the old oak tree in our backyard—I'd screamed. Running for cover as a giant tree limb fell right where I had been standing. Frozen in panic, all I could do was cover my head and huddle under the oak tree.

I'd cried and cried, not knowing that my father was frantically searching for me from the porch. I wouldn't have been able to hear him over my sobs anyway. By the time the storm quieted, my father was knocking on neighbors' doors and asking if they had seen me, his worries scrawled onto a damp piece of paper. He couldn't sign fast enough that he needed help.

It was Mason's mother who found me, she'd heard me crying. There had been a scolding later that day after my father's relief subsided. A scolding because I hadn't abided by the one rule of respect we were to show him—I hadn't told him I was going outside.

Ever since that day, lightning and thunder could raise the hairs on the back of my neck. In the flash of a moment, I could become that eight-year-old girl again. So alone, so afraid.

It just so happened that storms in Scotland were a little more powerful than at home. While I didn't have to worry about tree limbs near the coast, everything here was louder—the rush of the wind and the rain, the booming gong of the thunder, sometimes rumbling, and sometimes cracking like the sharp snap of a tree—forcing me into a huddled ball beneath the blankets. For what felt like hours, I played soft music, but it was often lost in the storm. I hummed, tried reading, but nothing helped.

Was it getting louder?

I didn't know if that was even possible, but it seemed like it was.

Enough was enough. Feeling like a child, I creeped to the door and out into the hall. I'd already checked twice to see if Roland's light was on, but it wasn't. I don't know why I expected it to be this time. Slinking closer, I wondered if I should knock. Being alone during a storm was my least favorite thing. It was part of the reason I had gotten Chandler. He'd made it easier for me to maintain some semblance of courage. Simply having another heartbeat around the house was enough to calm the fears that I never could fully overcome.

Inhaling deeply, I crept closer to Roland's door. Two kinds of fear roiled within me. One, the fear of what had been coursing between us on the beach. The other, this storm. I wondered which would win out when a crack of thunder rattled the windows again.

My hand raised of its own accord. I hated that I had tears in my eyes. I was a grown woman for crying out loud. This shouldn't affect me the way it did.

I wouldn't let it.

Determined, I turned away from Roland's door and tiptoed back toward my guest room. The wood creaked beneath my feet and when a shudder of lighting illuminated the hallway, I braced myself against the wall in anticipation of the thunder. Even though I was prepared, I still couldn't stop my hand from flying to my throat as the power of the storm seemed to rattle the entire house.

Deep breaths, come on now, just breathe.

"Dani?"

I hadn't heard him open the door and I didn't even look at him, so pure was my terror. I ran for his room like a caged animal raced for freedom. My shoulder smacked into the door frame and I sucked in a shocked breath, pain radiating along my arm. That was going to leave a bruise.

"That had to hurt," Roland mumbled, his voice groggy with sleep.

I didn't answer and wrapped my arms around my body, my hands were shaking. Another deep breath and I was letting some of my fears go, when another rumble of thunder trembled, making me quake where I stood.

"Dani?" Roland said again, this time his voice had changed. I couldn't even look at him. Warm fingers touched my shoulder and drew me to him. In a step he had me in his arms, my face pressed against his sweatshirt, his hands rubbing up and down my back. Tears welled in my eyes.

"I'm sorry," I murmured. "I should be over this by now. It's just so loud here."

"Don't apologize." He murmured and I felt a slight pressure on the top of my head. His lips? "You're trembling." It wasn't an accusation, just a fact. "I should have checked on you earlier."

"You didn't know." I was breathless.

"I almost did check," he admitted and then drew back slightly, one arm still wrapped around me, the other creeping between us to tilt my chin up. His eyes searched mine. "I didn't realize it still bothered you so much."

It shouldn't surprise me that Roland understood my fears. He was the one who had sat with me in my car when a lightning storm had canceled a high school football game. I'd been too afraid to drive home. He'd offered and I'd declined—too afraid to move.

I'd told him that night, at sixteen, that I still felt like a terrified child— forever lost to the world when I wasn't at home during a storm. It had happened one other time too, during a summer in college, but I'd told him then I was fine. He'd still hurried me home, and all night I had debated calling him. He hadn't known I was the only one in the house.

I'd spent most of the night fretting—especially when the power went out, but I had made it through. It had been my fault for not being honest with him, for not telling him I didn't want to be alone during a storm. The next morning I'd searched for puppies and later that week brought Chandler home.

Chandler, lazy though he was, had been my line of defense for years. But I didn't have him with me here. Instead, I had Roland—who was proving to be a much better comforter than my sleepy dog.

Inhaling, I leaned into Roland's hand that caressed my face again. On the beach, I'd pulled away—the two parts of myself warring within me. But here, now, I didn't have the strength to fight.

Had it always been this way between us? Had I always wanted to be this close to him? I breathed; uncertain I could trust what was so easily coursing through me. I reached deep within, trying to find the wall that had always rested between us. There were only a few stones left, but I could stand there, couldn't I?

Maybe I could hold firm.

A shiver raced down my spine, only this time it had nothing to do with fear. Something new was taking over.

"Are you cold?" Roland drew back, misinterpreting my trembling.

"No," I said, attempting to hold him in place, but he moved anyway. Suddenly I was cold, the warmth of him still lingering on my fingers.

I watched as he opened a drawer in his dresser and pulled out a long sleeve shirt. With one swift move he pulled the sweatshirt he was wearing over his head. There he stood, his plaid pajama pants resting low on his hips and it was all I could do not to stare.

A million thoughts flew through my mind at once. Given our growing up together, I'd seen him shirtless countless times around pools and trips to the beach. But adulthood had given away to work, and lazy days at the pool had disappeared as quickly as a sunset.

I hadn't seen him like this in years.

Correction. I'd never seen him like this.

Shirtless, all masculine and so close I could reach him. My heart pounded and when the thunder rumbled above, I blinked quickly as though just now realizing I had been staring, letting my eyes snake along the lines of his broad chest and the flatness of his stomach.

He held the sweatshirt out to me and I snatched it without protest. I wasn't sure if I would even be able to talk if I tried.

Throwing on his sweatshirt, I tried to tamper down the piece of me that was reveling in this. I would keep my wits about me, I had to. Too much rested on this. Our friendship was too much to gamble away.

Instead of enjoying this, I would tell myself what not to do. Like how I would not notice how big and warm his sweatshirt was, and I would not allow myself to think about the fact that he had been sleeping in it moments ago. I also would not allow my eyes to watch the way his muscles rippled and moved as he put on the long sleeve shirt he'd pulled from the dresser. And I refused to acknowledge the way the collar parted slightly at the top revealing the smooth lines of his neck.

Instead, I would focus on the logo on the front of the sweatshirt. It was gray with the Scottish flag beneath the word 'Culloden.' I fingered the fabric, waiting for Roland to say something and to not be so aware of him. It took only a moment for me to realize I was failing miserably on all accounts. I cleared my throat, fidgeting. A masculine, almost wooded scent from his clothes filled my nose.

Light from outside flashed, illuminating the room before it grew dark again. Perhaps Roland came to the same conclusion and realized how at odds we were in the dark. How different everything was. He moved to turn on a lamp.

I blinked at the golden glow and as my eyes adjusted, remained awkwardly standing on the rug beside the bed. The covers were flipped back as though he had rushed to find me.

"What now?" I whispered, uncertain. Was he longing to close the distance between us too?

He laughed, an almost breathless sound, and shook his head. Color flooded his cheeks and he wouldn't meet my gaze. It helped to know he was as unsteady as me, on the beach he had seemed more than in control.

"Do you want a glass of wine?"

I pursed my lips, it did sound nice, but I knew he wouldn't join me. Thinking of his father, I shook my head.

"Hot chocolate?"

That was better—safer. "Sure, but won't your Nan and Pap wake up?"

"In this storm?" One dark eyebrow rose. "They don't sleep with their hearing aids. We can throw a party if we want."

"Maybe tomorrow night."

"Perfect," he grinned, that crooked smile warming me like his sweatshirt. "I'll be right back."

He left then, and I was alone once more, only this time it didn't feel the same. Somehow knowing he would return helped to drown out the roar of the storm. Not knowing what else to do, I perched on the edge of the bed and waited, folding my legs up beneath me so my toes would catch some warmth beneath the blankets.

When he returned, he held up the mugs as though in triumph. Thunder rattled the windows as I held the cup against my cheek for warmth. Shifting back, I leaned against the headboard, watching as he moved to the wooden chair in the room. He rested his crossed ankles on the mattress.

"Can they sleep through this?" I pointed a finger upward.

He nodded. "I was."

"Oh?" Somehow, knowing he'd been asleep made sitting on his bed all the more intimate. Or maybe it was that the blankets were mussed and not carefully tucked in order.

"And I'm guessing you haven't slept at all."

"What tipped you off?" I rolled my eyes, sarcasm was easier—this was normal for us. "Was it my shaking hands, or the fact that I was probably as white as a ghost?"

"Actually, it was you running in here faster than I've ever seen you move, that's when I thought maybe something isn't right." He smiled then, the creases around his mouth so familiar to me.

I understood this—this kinship that brought us close but remained on the side of the wall that was familiar. That other side was a question mark, a closeness, and intimacy that I was too afraid to explore.

"So," I said, growing with confidence now that my feet were on solid ground. "What should we do?"

Roland shrugged and then attempted to reach for his phone on the bedside table. For a moment he looked as though he might fall off his chair, that or drop the mug, but as his fingers scrambled for purchase, he finally pulled his phone closer. I rolled my eyes and made sure he saw it.

"Best of the '90s?" he asked, scrolling. "Or maybe the 2000's?"

Soon music from our later high school years was playing gently from his speaker. So many memories wrapped up into songs. Before long we were reminiscing. Talking about those times when life was simpler, full of opportunities and question marks on where our lives would lead. I missed that feeling, and yet, I loved being where I was. Just because the hands of time had turned didn't mean my life was any more certain.

Growing up it often felt like those who were older had their lives all in order, that they were so certain, so assured. But the longer I lived the more I realized everyone was just taking it one day at a time—and no more certain than they were as teenagers.

Perhaps the easiest way to handle it all was to just accept life for the question mark it was—an adventure of unknowns.

"Remember the hot wings?" I started laughing before Roland had even finished talking. Our school had tried to introduce hot wings as an option for lunch. The pranks were endless, boys swapping out regular wings for hot, bring hot sauce with them to spice it up even more—it hadn't taken long for them to disappear.

"Kari didn't see that one coming," I chortled and then snorted, making both of us laugh even harder. I sighed heavily. "Those were good times."

The song changed and I perked up. "Yes! This is my jam!"

"Jam? What are you, forty?"

"Yes, I'm turning forty next year," I would have rolled my eyes, but I was already moving my head to the beat.

"You're ridiculous," Roland laughed, but I didn't care.

Maybe it was the release of the tension that had been holding me captive through most of the night, or maybe it was just being here with him, but I threw inhibitions to the wind. Bobbing my head to the music I stood, putting my empty mug to the side. As the beat picked up, I shimmied my shoulders and hopped around to the beat. Roland was laughing but I didn't care as I grabbed his hand and pulled him to his feet.

Fun had no age limit.

All it took was a few tugs before he was swinging me around too. If there was one thing Roland was good at, it was dancing. He'd told me his mom needed a partner to practice with—she ballroom danced as a hobby and he'd been learning all the moves since he was ten.

He swung me around, our rhythm completely off from the music, but I didn't care. I was all things light and carefree.

As the beat built to the last chorus we hopped up and down and I half-tripped, half fell on the bed. He pulled me back to my feet and we finished out the song dancing across from one another, my arms attempting something like the wave, while he did the running man.

A cackle escaped me and I covered my mouth with my hand. "There's no way they aren't awake now."

"Shhh," Roland said, the hypocrite talking even louder than I was. "we probably should turn it down."

"Has the rain stopped?" As though in answer a roaring whir rushed against the windows. "At least tell me their bedroom is on the other side of the house."

He nodded as a rumble of thunder rolled overhead. It sounded as though it was finally moving on, the storm not as close as it had been.

I was sweating, only slightly, but I loved the way my heart was pounding in my chest. The next song was just as familiar, even if the beat was slower. I shifted slightly, moving to the rhythm of the music almost subconsciously. From somewhere in the back of my mind, I remembered hearing this song at prom, I remembered dancing in a group as it boomed through the speakers.

When I turned back to Roland, I found him watching me. There was that look again—the one that could so easily undo me. Undo our past.

My heart shuttered—trembled as I stopped dancing. Fingering the edge of his too-large sweatshirt, I met his gaze. He didn't move, but I did.

I reached him as the song changed, as it morphed into a slow, persistent beat. It sounded like longing to me.

When I stepped in front of him, all smiles had faded. The same tension that had coursed between us on the beach returned. He was all I could see, and all our life seemed to be leading to this. I was weak and strong all at once.

Idly, I reached for his hands, entwining my fingers with his, slowly, gently. I thought I heard his breath hitch as I moved toward his wrist and up his arms—all of this was so new, so strange. We'd come so far, and yet not far enough.

I thought of all the things I had told him—the deepest parts of me—and he was still here. I'd confessed to him my longing to be loved, to be seen—my fears of being like Charlotte Lucas. I'd feared being overlooked, but I hadn't realized he'd been the one to see me all along.

So, what was I waiting for?

We'd never done this, never crossed this line—but maybe we could.

Running my hands up his forearms, I touched his biceps and slowly, ever so slowly, reached for his shoulders. It was then that I looked up and my breath caught. All lightheartedness had fled, all uncertainty had faded. There in Roland's eyes was the emotion that had always been lingering.

Restraint fled. In his eyes was love and care, unbridled passion and it warmed me in a way I hadn't thought possible. The short strands of his hair fell from around his ears and framed his face as he gazed down at me. I pushed his hair back, remembering how it had felt the night I ran my fingers through it.

My mere touch seemed to snap whatever had frozen him and he shifted, taking control. His hands tightened around my waist and drew me closer as my fingers played with the strands of hair at the nape of his neck. I don't know if it was the feel of his arms holding me close or the look in his eyes, but I inhaled sharply and his gaze drifted to my lips.

"I don't know how to be like this with you," I admitted in a breathless whisper.

"Neither do I."

His confession gave me courage. Heart pounding in my ears, I spoke. "But I want to."

He wasted no time, his head dipping until, quite suddenly, his mouth claimed mine.

It was passion and longing. It was desire—expressed in the press of his lips on mine. When I clung to him, pressing closer to his chest, he groaned and his lips became insistent, almost feverish. I suddenly felt the wall at my back as he pushed me into it.

His hands framed my face, tilting my head exactly how he wanted it, parting my lips in a way that had me growing weak. I had never known it could be like this—that this burning fire could grow even stronger. It was as though every thought I'd pushed aside, every inkling I'd held off over the years was suddenly released in the crumbling of the wall between us.

My feelings for him crested in a wave, only to be toppled by another as I inhaled the masculine scent enveloping me. I sighed his name more than once and when he drew back to look down at me, I wondered how we had never done this before. How had I never seen him this way?

I was breathing heavily, almost embarrassingly and my hands which were on his chest rose and fell with each of his breaths.

He lowered his forehead to mine and there were no words as his thumbs brushed gently against my cheeks. And then he dipped his head again, as though he couldn't stand the distance either.

His mouth moved against mine, gently at first, and then almost powerfully, desperately. He wrapped his arms around me, drawing me even closer. I'd been right before; he knew exactly what he was doing.

Time faded and for how long we remained, I didn't know, but all too soon he drew back. I was trembling—this time for a different reason.

When we broke apart, it was with heavy breaths that turned to smiles. Roland pressed his lips to my forehead, and I suddenly remembered I was standing. All thought but him had left me for however long we had kissed.

"Dani," he sighed, and when he pulled me into his arms, I tucked my chin and leaned into the strength of his chest. There were many parts of this that could ruin what we had, but I didn't have the capacity to think about them right now.

At this moment I needed something more, I needed him, I needed the idea of us to just linger.

"I've wanted to do that for a long time," Roland said, his deep voice rumbling in his chest.

My lips curved at his confession. I didn't have any words to describe what was going through my mind—what was searing my heart. It was like the breaking of dawn, this shining light cresting the horizon so quickly that I didn't know how I'd never seen it before.

The music changed again. Gently, we began to shift slowly from side to side. The heat of the moment fading into a closeness that touched my soul. Was this what love was? I didn't know. All I knew was longing and pain, the unrecognized yearning for someone who could never be.

I'd loved Roland for years, was it possible that this love of friendship had transformed without my knowledge? That it had taken shape without my approval?

I tightened my hold around Roland's waist. "I think I just won."

"Hmmm?" The timbre of his voice rumbled in his chest. It warmed me to hear how fast his heart was still beating.

"You're a romantic after all, Roland Harmon."

"I could put Mr. Darcy to shame."

We both laughed softly, almost sleepily as the rain still poured in heavy torrents on the roof above us. Roland's hands gently rubbed against my back and I knew that this was a moment and a feeling I wanted to remember. Wrapped in his arms, wearing his sweatshirt, I still didn't know what it all meant, but I wanted to.

When I yawned, Roland felt the shiver that ran through me. I'd forgotten how cold it was in his room since we were standing so close. When he wrapped a blanket around my shoulders, I pulled away from him and crawled onto the bed, sitting with my back against the headboard. As though it was the most natural thing, and something we had done hundreds of times, Roland climbed in beside me, drawing me close under his arm.

The heaping rolls of thunder had faded into the background, their declarations having lost their strength now that I was with Roland. Yawning again, I tucked myself closer to his side, a part of me wondering if this was all a dream. It felt like the most natural thing in the world, and yet it wasn't.

But I would worry about that tomorrow. For now, I synchronized my breath with his, not caring about what the morning would bring. Ever so slowly, my eyes grew weighted and as I drifted off, I thought I heard him whisper.

"Goodnight, Dani."

CHAPTER 22

Had Charlotte Lucas ever experienced the warmth of being curled up beside a man? Did she ever get the chance to know what it felt like to smile upon waking, to feel so secure beneath the heavy, slumbering arm of the man at her back?

I hoped she had—even if she was fictional—because it was a pleasure unlike any other. A secure and comforting place that I never wanted to leave.

At some point during the night, the rain had faded. The silence was almost overwhelming, making me feel everything all at once—the rise and fall of the blankets, our steady deep breaths, the warmth radiating from the body behind mine. His chest was pressed securely against my back, my body curled into his.

As the fog of morning drifted, my sluggish thoughts assembled. And when they did, my eyes flew open in surprise. *Roland.*

I had known he was there, that we lay in the same bed, but to know and *really* know were two very different things. It seemed so right to be here like this with him. To simply be—and yet, I didn't know what to do now that I was aware of it.

The wall between us had shattered. Whatever boundary lines we'd put in place years ago had disappeared. I was laid bare, and somehow it was at once terrifying and wonderful. A mix of daring and joy.

Shifting ever so slightly, Roland's arm tightened in sleep as though to pull me closer.

Everything was a muddled mess. If I needed any proof of what had passed between us, last night, this was it. Memories of his lips on mine brought a smile to my face—even as heat flooded my cheeks.

The memory burned, scorched into my mind, into my soul.

It had seemed so right, so natural. Was it possible I had wanted to be like this with him all along?

After waiting for Roland to wake up for what felt like an hour, I shifted from under his arm. Nothing could have prepared me for the sight of him, his hair mussed on the pillow, his mouth slack and his lips parted slightly.

Leaning down, I placed a kiss on his cheek and watched as his mouth drew back slightly in a smile before his breathing grew deeper. Warmth seeped into my heart, spreading to every part of me.

Perhaps I had been blind for far too long.

Leaving his room, I hastened to change, deciding to keep his sweatshirt. He might as well resign to the fact that I might confiscate it for life.

"Good morning, dear." So lost in thought, I almost cried out in surprise when Nan greeted me from the kitchen.

"Go-oo-d morning," I fumbled for words.

"I hope you were able to get some sleep last night."

Blushing like a schoolgirl, I nodded. "Yes."

"Quite a storm. We haven't had one like that in ages."

I nodded, hating how embarrassed and distracted I was.

"We're going for a walk in a minute if you would like to join us," Nan offered. Only now did I realize she had her boots laced and a heavy coat zipped up to her chin. Fresh air sounded wonderful.

I nodded again and tried to ignore the curious smile she gave me. I would pretend I hadn't seen that—and assume she was simply having a good morning. I didn't want to know if she presumed anything. How could she? I didn't even know what was going on in my own heart.

Only when Pap rounded the corner and took in my sweatshirt, did I realize my mistake. He sent his wife a curious look that had her smiling even broader. They couldn't have been more obvious if they tried.

Blushing, I rushed back up the stairs to grab my coat and boots—partially to gather my courage at being alone with them, and in part to give them the chance to get their presumptions out in the open.

The temperature had dropped during the night, if such a thing was possible, the wind sharp and tugging at my hair. I knew I would miss the pulsing energy of the air when I returned home. In Landing, there were breezes that cooled, fresh winds of calming relaxation, but here the wind was tinged with anticipation. A sense of nagging enticement that made me want to explore—to cast off all fears and worries which too often held me back.

We reached the beach without a word spoken between us. The sand was dented with little divots—evidence of what had transpired in the night. The waves seemed to have spent their energy, their efforts lazy as they lapped against the shore. Was it only yesterday that Roland and I had raced the horses across the sand?

Why was everything so confusing? It all felt so right, but it was the plot twist I'd never expected. I needed to talk to someone.

Thinking of my older sister, Anna, I wished I'd thought to message her this morning. Although, given the time change she was more than likely passed out or nursing in the middle of the night. Regardless, she would know what to do, she would know what to say. I'd clearly done enough to confuse myself when it came to understanding this new thing forming between me and Roland.

Anna knew all about Mason, she knew every detail and had answered so many late-night texts. I would have to send her a message about all of this when we returned. Somehow, she always knew what to say.

Nan and Pap turned off of the beach and began to climb up the small hill toward the cresting rocks. I followed, loving the way the Scottish wind lifted my hair. I would miss this place when Roland and I left.

Perhaps he was right, my heart did belong here.

"So, tell me Dani, has Scotland lived up to your expectations?"

I nearly laughed. How could I tell Roland's grandfather that Scotland had turned out to be the most unexpected breath of fresh air I never knew I needed?

"Oh, it's been even better."

"Good," he nodded. He walked with his hands swinging gently at his sides. I could already tell he enjoyed the walk, while Nan was working up a sweat. She was about ten steps in front of us. I liked how their personalities were so different and yet, in synch.

"It's so beautiful," I admitted. "What made you guys decide to retire here." I had often wondered about that. They obviously enjoyed spending time with Roland, so why live so far away from him and their daughter-in-law?

Pap took some time before answering, his steps slowing. I worried I had said something wrong. "You don't have to answer that," I offered.

He waved a hand. "No, no, I was just waiting until my darling was further ahead." He winked at me and then glanced back at Nan, she was now at least twenty steps in front of us. "Scotland was James's favorite."

It all clicked. Roland had told me his dad was an avid traveler. "Oh," was all I could think to say.

Pap nodded. "Roland tries so hard to not be like his dad sometimes, and because of that he is like him in many ways."

"I get that." My breaths were coming in sharper gasps than they should have as we crested the top of the hill. "Sometimes that happens. I went through a rebellious phase when I was in middle school. I wanted to be nothing like my older sister, not because I didn't like her but because I knew I couldn't be so perfect."

"Ahh, sibling rivalry."

"Exactly," I grinned. Pap was easy to talk to. Something his grandson had inherited. I wondered if James had been that way. "Anna has always been the strong one in our family, but if you asked her, she wouldn't consider herself that way."

"Why's that?"

"Because she's always been humble, something I am lacking in many ways."

"Isn't the first step admitting you have a problem?" Pap chuckled and I grinned.

"You've got me there."

We walked in silence for a few minutes and I could feel the weight of his thoughts— a deep furrow wrinkled his brow. A part of me wondered if this was how Roland would look when he reached his grandfather's age. It was easy to imagine, Roland morphing into something like this kind man in the years to come.

I wondered if I would be there to see it. Thinking of last night my lips tingled. That lingering something loomed on the horizon.

"We traveled a lot with James when he was young. My wife has those wandering bones in her body," Pap kept his gaze on his feet as we walked, but his voice was calm, assertive, "she blames herself for the way James left his family."

It was my turn to be confused. "But she never left both of you."

"If there's one thing I have learned about women it is that they will always blame themselves for the things that happen to their children. The 'What if's' can be all too consuming."

I nodded as though I understood, but I couldn't, not really. I thought of Anna and wondered if this was how she felt about her children. And I thought of my mother. She knew how I felt about still being single, about how life had turned out to be so very different than I expected or wanted, was it possible she blamed herself for pieces of it? Even thinking such a thought made me flinch.

"Roland has told us a lot about you over the years," Pap's words broke through my thoughts.

The change in topic nearly drew me up short. I didn't know how to answer, so I didn't.

"We hoped we would get the chance to meet you someday."

"I hoped the same about both of you. He talks about you guys all the time."

Pap grinned and those same lines that Roland had around his mouth creased. "That's kind of you to say."

I squinted up at him. Though the day was overcast, it was still bright.

Up ahead I saw Nan turn to the left. Pap chuckled, seemingly to himself. "Thank goodness you're walking with me. Gives me an excuse to walk slowly. Normally she yells at me to hurry up."

I laughed. "I will gladly be your scapegoat for as long as we're here."

"Have you ever been fishing? Roland and I are planning to go again. Why don't you join us?"

That was an invitation I couldn't pass up. "I'd love to."

"Now we just have to wait for her legs to get tired and then we can go wake up Roland."

The mention of Roland made my stomach flip on itself. Change was certainly upon us.

Turns out, I was no great fisher. A fact that Roland and his Pap tried to remedy, much to their good humor. I was relieved upon returning to the house after our walk to find Roland dressed and ready for the day. Somehow seeing him outside the house and in the open-air allowed me the chance to breathe easier. Last night could be tucked into a corner of my mind for the time being—I would deal with it later.

Of course, it didn't stop my heart from flipping every time he touched me. It was as though our kiss had awakened every cell in my body, making me overly aware of him and each brush of his hand on mine, or his fingers gripping my waist or wrists to help me reel in a fish, left a lingering warmth across my skin.

After a few pleasant hours on the boat, and a hasty lunch of sandwiches, we returned to the house to clean up for dinner. Nan and Pap had invited us to join them in town for dinner at a local pub.

Later when we were into a booth at the pub, live singers performed for those in attendance. A man was playing guitar as a woman with a deep, throaty voice sang alluring and beautiful folk songs. I found my feet tapping along to their music, especially on the ones that seemed to be pub favorites. Some of the locals called out requests and the man would just smile and turn to the woman before starting up his guitar.

At times we clapped along, and I found myself completely content with the atmosphere as our food was served and eaten. Nan and Pap left the table every now and then to mingle with some of their friends.

I sighed; all was right in the world.

Tucked into the back corner of the booth, I smiled as another song began, the dim light lulling me into a state of contentment. "This has been just perfect."

Roland sat beside me, his arm touching mine, where we could view the stage from our table. "I know."

"No, really," I said, turning to look at him fully. "I needed this, this whole trip. More than I knew."

The side of his mouth quirked and he looked down at his hands resting on the table. Thinking of last night again, I tested the newness between us. Around others, we were the same as we had always been, but alone, it was new. There was a depth to this friendship that I'd never experienced before. A crossing of distances that couldn't be explained in tangible words, but could be measured in light touches, in probing questions, and the subtle changes in breath.

With him, alone, the world seemed to slow down.

But the nagging fear remained. Could I do this? Could I explore what was between us?

To jump so far from the wall could kill us both.

What rested between us felt like glass, or ice—it could crack easily and if I fell in, I didn't know if I would be able to swim.

Perhaps I was too much like Charlotte Lucas. I was too afraid to search for something that would ignite my heart. Fear kept me trapped in that which I understood. Friendship with Roland was comfortable. What had come over us last night was new, enticing, and yet dangerous. I didn't understand it and was therefore afraid.

Mayhap it was Scotland and the seemingly magical spirits that had changed my view of Roland. Maybe if I set my mind on being his friend again tonight, I could overcome the fear and simply allow things to happen as they should.

Putting Charlotte Lucas from my mind, I leaned my head back against the wall and allowed the live music to still the chaotic twirl of my thoughts. Crossing my arms, I angled my body so I could see Roland more clearly.

"How are Anna and Henry?" he asked.

My eyebrows rose at the mention of my siblings. "Good. Anna is busy with the new baby, he's so cute." Roland smiled at that. "And Henry is liking his job."

"North Carolina, right?"

I nodded. "Yeah, Ashville area."

"Maybe we should go visit the Biltmore."

"Maybe, I've always wanted to go, but I think it is going to pale in comparison to all this."

Roland gave another smile; one I couldn't entirely read. "Nan said you're welcome to come back anytime. I don't think it matters if I'm with you."

I laughed, rolling my eyes. "Doubtful."

"That's what she told me," he held his hands up in innocent surrender.

"I think they would be sorely disappointed if it was just me." A lingering thought nagged "How come your mom never visits with you?"

Roland inhaled a deep breath. "She has once or twice, but she doesn't really like flying. And I think Pap reminds her too much of my dad."

I nodded. "I could see that."

His brow furrowed as he turned to me. "Oh, you can, can you?"

"Come on, you're like the spitting image of him. Same eyes, you both furrow your brow the same way, yes like that, and then you smile the same too. You get these lines around your mouth." I gestured around my own and watched as his gaze dropped, lingering for a moment on my lips.

It was suddenly very warm in our corner of the booth. The intensity of his gaze reminded me too much of last night and how it had felt to have his mouth against mine.

Drawing back from that thought, I ran a hand through my hair and focused on the singers on stage. If I really concentrated, I could tap my foot to the beat. It was only when I glanced his way that I faltered. Roland was still watching me—his mouth lined in seriousness, but his eyes warm, drawing me in. As the minutes ticked by he shifted, looking toward the stage. I took a breath of relief.

Pretending to simply be friends was going to prove much harder than I had thought.

"Do you have any pictures of Jackson?" he asked.

I nodded, nearly jumping at the offer to change the subject. My youngest nephew was only a few months old and I received pictures of him, my niece, and the other two nephews almost daily.

Unlocking my phone, I frowned. Mason had messaged me again. I swiped it aside, seeing how long the message was. No doubt some update on the situation with Nancy.

Swiping to my messages with Anna, I flipped through the pictures of Jackson. The one of him in mid-crumple on the couch while the other kids smiled, their grins straining their faces had Roland laughing.

"Anna said he almost fell off the couch, but he ended up just face planting into the cushions. As you can see, he gave the boys a laugh." I smiled down at their faces, one part surprise, the other part amused. Jackson wouldn't live this one down. Lucky for him, he was currently too young to understand.

"What are big brothers for," Roland chuckled.

"Yes," I clicked my phone off. "Did you ever wish you had siblings growing up?"

He shrugged. "Sometimes." He played with an empty straw wrapper on the table. "I always thought it would have been fun to have a younger sister or brother. Before we moved to Landing there were a few families we were close with. One of them had six kids—I loved going over to their house for dinner. It was like controlled chaos on taco night. All the dishes being passed back and forth. You had to eat with one hand and keep the other free for passing."

This glimpse into Roland's memories had me smiling. "Do you still keep in touch with them?"

He shrugged. "You know how it is, you see pictures on social media and comment every now and then. Sometimes Jen sends me a message, but that's only every six months or so."

Jen? I'd never heard of him talk of this childhood friend. Roland glanced up and laughed.

"Don't worry, Jen is happily married with five young children of her own."

I blinked. "I wasn't…"

It was his turn to roll his eyes. "You were, but that's okay." The thought seemed to please him. I blushed.

A smattering of applause interrupted us as the singers finished another song. They exited the makeshift stage and three men stood from a corner in the pub. They approached the microphones one with a guitar, the other holding a flute of some kind and the last one took a seat on a box. A few of the pub-goers shouted out some chants as the men adjusted their seats—the energy in the room rising.

"You're going to like this," Roland said softly.

I was already leaning a little further onto the table to get a better view. It grew strangely silent, the thrum of conversations dying as we all seemed to gather a breath together, waiting.

The man with the guitar leaned toward the microphone, his burly chest covered in a grey buttoned vest that matched his thick beard and the hair that reached his shoulders. He said something into the microphone that I couldn't understand. This was a different breed of Scottish, the accent so strong I wondered if he was speaking a different language. Glancing around I seemed to be the only one confused.

The crowd laughed at some joke before the drummer started thumping the box he sat on. And just like that my foot started tapping along and the man with the flute joined in and then the guitar took off. Before I knew it we were all clapping and singing along, or at least I was trying to sing.

Nan and Pap came back to join us and together we drank and talked, laughed, and listened to the folk songs that trilled throughout the pub. I was fairly certain that after all of this, Landing was going to seem quite dull.

It could have been five minutes or an hour later when the music stopped and we all clapped and cheered. After a resounding encore where the drummer went into a solo, the beat moving so quickly I could hardly keep up, the night came to an end and we made our way back to the house.

My heart was content, fears idling like the engine of the car as Pap pulled into the driveway and paused.

"What a great night," he said, and I couldn't have agreed more.

CHAPTER 23

There was a soft knock on my bedroom door not long after we said goodnight to Nan and Pap. My heart stuttered.

Taking a deep breath, I crossed the room and cracked open the door.

Roland was looking down at me, a burning question in his eyes—a question I wasn't sure I was ready to answer. "I want to show you something," he whispered.

I swallowed, uncertain and yet knowing I would go without question.

Throwing my coat back over my shoulders, I followed him down the stairs and out into the darkness of the frigid night. Roland reached for my hand, his own so warm around my fingers. I could feel how natural this would be. How easily we could continue from where we had started last night.

This was a different Roland than the one in the pub. This was the new side of him, the side I had seen as he took control in his room last night. The man who was so many things I didn't know and didn't fully understand.

My boots slipped in the sand, unstable like my thoughts which collided with one another. Grasping his hand a little tighter, I kept my eyes down and followed him, shivering as the wind cut through my coat. Each of my breaths became a cloud that quickly dissipated.

He came to a stop and I looked around, appreciating the lapping of the waves and the rush of wind. I wanted to look at Roland to see what he was thinking, feeling, but I wasn't sure if I wanted to see what was there. Fearing the answer, I remained focused on the horizon trying to muster some courage into my heart.

Out here I felt too exposed—too vulnerable.

A door had been opened that could no longer shut. It would either remain that way or be torn down, there was no going back to the way we were before we had kissed. The deal was struck.

The very thought sent a tremor along my spine. It was all too fast. Too much.

Roland squeezed my fingers. He might as well have squeezed my heart.

"Look," he whispered.

I tilted my chin to see him, only to realize he was gazing at the sky. My eyes followed and I gasped.

The stars. They were so bright, their shimmering brilliance so insistent it felt as though I could reach out and touch them.

Another night flickered in my mind—a summer evening on a trampoline. Pushing against the tightening in my chest I tried to focus on the moment at hand. That summer night had been the moment I saw Roland as more than just a friend. The single tear on his cheek had caused me to realize that there was more to him than what he showed the world.

And here, now, with him in Scotland I knew it to be true. He was very much a man any woman would be lucky to have, but I didn't know if that could be me. Or if I even wanted it to be me.

We had crossed that line between friends and something more last night in the heat of a moment. I could feel it lingering between us, the unspoken question of what could be on the horizon.

"Tell me something I don't know about you," Roland murmured, just loud enough for me to hear. When he squeezed my fingers again, I wasn't sure if I would be able to speak.

I thought for a long time and glanced around us. My hands were growing cold and I let go of Roland's to fold my arms across my chest. Still looking up I said, "Jimmy Stewart and Dick Van Dyke are two of my favorite actors."

Roland laughed. "That was random."

"You asked."

"How come?"

I shrugged. "They just seem like good guys, and there is something about Dick Van Dyke that just always makes me smile."

"I can see that. Is it the dancing penguins?"

I laughed thinking of *Mary Poppins*, "All of it." I wouldn't admit to how many movies of his I'd seen, or that I could quote most of the *Dick Van Dyke Show* episodes. "He has a kind of innate joy. There aren't many people like that."

"True," Roland nodded beside me, still looking at the stars.

Here in the pitch of night, I could remember him from so many years ago. How we had remained still on that trampoline beside each other, while the off-key singing of our friends filled the night. Seeing him now was like looking into a window of the past.

"You're like that," I admitted, knowing it was true. He met my gaze, his eyes warming me in a way only his could. "Always positive, hopeful."

"Thank you for that." He turned toward me, and my stomach clenched, uncertainty hovering. When his hand reached for my cheek, I braced myself for what I would feel. This was unlike us, everything had changed.

I longed for steady ground, not this swirling ocean of emotion that threatened my stability.

"I want to tell you something," he said, and my stomach pinched painfully. His thumb continued to brush my cheek and I blinked quickly as the wall around my heart began to tremble, threatening to break. I didn't like having my emotions out of my control.

A blanket of fear shrouded me. I didn't know if I could do this. To do this would be to risk it all, and if the world had taught me anything it was that feelings weren't enough. Attraction wasn't enough. Love wasn't enough.

It had to be more than that.

Perhaps I was more like Charlotte Lucas than I had originally thought, more cynical and practical. But to be practical was to be safe. And to risk getting hurt was too much. I'd tried to take a leap with Mason and I couldn't even get off the ground. But the way that Roland was looking at me now was so hopeful that I didn't want to see it fall—I didn't want to be the reason our friendship collapsed, and yet we had never done this before. We didn't know what was on the other side of becoming something more.

Trepidation lingered and I wrapped it around me like a blanket. It would keep me on solid ground if I didn't change what was between us.

Roland placed both hands along the sides of my face, his eyes burning into mine. That smile lining his lips was enough to unsettle the beat of my heart. "Dani—"

"Don't," I butted in. It was the only word I could get past my lips.

He faltered. "Don't what?"

"Don't say anything," I swallowed heavily.

"Why not?" His eyes squinted, the hope dimming.

"Because I can't." My breath hitched on the last word.

"Can't what?"

"Be with you." There I had said it.

It took a moment for my words to register, but when they did, he blinked down at me, almost dazed, before his hands fell away from my face and reached my shoulders. Rather than turn away, he stepped closer peering into my eyes more seriously, as though he was searching for something there. Everything in me screamed for retreat.

"You're afraid," he said. He might as well have pulled my heart from my chest and laid it bare for the world to see.

"No," tears were in my voice. Why now must I cry?

"You are," he said with unbridled confidence. "You're afraid and that's why you're going to throw this away."

I turned my head to look out at the ocean. "No, no, no," I mumbled not wanting to believe it was true.

"Admit it," his words were almost forceful, and yet gentle, coaxing me, convincing me to see his side. But that was the problem, I did see his side, and it wasn't enough. He loved me, I knew it now, but I didn't know how I felt about him. And I couldn't be that person.

For years I had longed for Mason, I had hoped and prayed he would notice me, see me as someone worthy of his attention, but it had all been for naught. Mason and I were never to be, and I wouldn't be the one to drag Roland along. I couldn't.

If I knew that something more was possible, if I knew I loved him as more than a friend, then I could join him in this pursuit, but I wouldn't do it otherwise. I wouldn't be that person.

I was too afraid to let him take the leap and watch us fall.

"Admit what?"

"That you're afraid."

I shook my head. "No, I'm not."

"You are."

Tears prickled my eyes. "I just...can't." I was shaking my head. Roland's fingers tightened on my upper arms, his eyes piercing me. "I can't be the one for you."

He flinched, even though he tried to hide it. His hands fell away from my arms.

"Is this because of Mason?" he asked, never looking away.

"No," I wiped away a tear. Pieces of me were falling apart. I wasn't like this; I didn't cry in front of people.

"Really?" he challenged.

"Why would you even think that?"

"Come on, Dani. I've known how you felt about him for years, it's why I've never—" he broke off taking a shaking breath.

"It's why what? Why you encouraged me to tell him how I felt?" I snapped. Frustration seemed easier than facing the fear coursing within me. "Did you know that he was with Nancy when you told me to take a leap of faith?"

His brow furrowed, but it was the way he shifted that told me everything I needed to know.

"You knew?"

He nodded. "I knew they were together."

"And still you sent me to tell him how I felt?" My voice trembled, the sting of betrayal nearly overwhelming me.

"No!" he said quickly, running a hand through his hair. "That's not what—I wasn't—" he mumbled something under his breath and looked at our boots in the sand. "I didn't know you were going to take my advice that way. This is all so messed up. I meant for you to do something for yourself, to take Mrs. Kent's offer, and not be afraid for once."

His words slid everything into place. Even Roland hadn't expected me to ever be with Mason. Perhaps the whole world could see it and I couldn't. It no longer mattered, I knew now it would never happen, but that near leap had been one of the bravest things I'd ever done.

"Sorry to disappoint," I said and turned from him slightly, unable to fully comprehend the way Roland saw me. He viewed me as a coward—someone who was too afraid to go for what she wanted. And he was right, and because of that, it was nearly my undoing.

"Dani," he sighed. "You did it though, you made the trip. You took that leap—be proud of yourself."

"Proud?" I gave a sharp laugh. "How can I be proud? I didn't do this because I was brave. I was running away, Roland. Don't you understand that? I was running away from my feelings for Mason, my disappointed hopes, and my fears of being alone. I decided to run away and the worst part is all of it will be there waiting for me when I get home."

Silence met my outburst.

A sharp wind pulled at my hair and I sniffed, hoping it was the cold night that was making my nose run, but I knew it wasn't. I was one of those people who seemed to create exorbitant amounts of snot when I cried. It was truly terrifying and the main reason I only cried alone.

"This just isn't real life Roland."

That seemed to pull him from his thoughts. "What is?"

"This," I gestured around me, "coming to Scotland, visiting Pemberley, all of it. It's a fantasy. Real life is hard and things don't change so fast. This," I waved a hand between us, "is happening too fast. It's not real. It's just, it's too fast."

Roland closed the distance between us, his jaw tightening. There was a determination in his eyes that I had never seen before. "No, this is real. It's you and me. We've been this way for years and you've just been too blind to see it. It's been this way since we met, Dani." His voice broke slightly on my name and I suddenly knew I was hurting him.

This was a different kind of pain, the kind I knew so well. I'd been the one to long for another, to feel invisible, to be unseen. How had I never realized what I'd been doing to Roland? How had I never noticed? I was no better than Mason.

"I'm scared." The admission nearly took all of me. Why couldn't I overcome this wall around my heart?

"Of what," he wrapped his arms around me. The dark strands of his hair rippled in the wind. "Of me? Of us?"

I nodded. "The idea of us. It's too fast. I don't know if I can be who you need me to be."

He was already shaking his head, "You don't have to be anyone but you, Dani. I've loved you since high school." He placed a kiss on my forehead, his lips lingering. I stared at my fingers curled against the warmth of his chest. He lifted my chin until my gaze met his. "We can do this together for however long it takes, we can go on this adventure."

He stared into my eyes, his own hopeful.

Then like a wave crashing on the shore, I watched as his expression fell. For a moment I didn't know what had happened. Had I said something? Done something?

All of me felt laid bare before him—what more could he have seen?

Slowly his arms slipped from around my body, his expression one of shock. "I've been wrong this whole time, haven't I?" he asked, staring at our entwined fingers, defeated.

"I—I don't understand," I mumbled. The urge to lean into him again was nearly overwhelming.

Roland's breath caught and I suddenly realized he was about to cry. I had heard his breath hitch like that once before.

"Do you remember the bonfire before all of you left for college?"

I nearly froze. When I didn't respond he continued.

"I overheard what you told Kari that night." He looked toward the ocean, a muscle in his jaw clenched, the light of the stars glimmering in his eyes. Were those tears? My eyes welled up as I knew I was somehow the reason for his pain.

What could I have done? Thinking back on that night, I couldn't remember anything but blurred glimpses of dancing around the bonfire and singing songs. The only solid and clear image was that tear on Roland's cheek.

"You told Kari that you wanted a life of adventure."

I blinked, not remembering if I had said that. It was true of the time. My dreams had been big and bold back then.

"You told her everything you hoped to do, the places you wanted to visit, and where you wanted to live. None of it had anything to do with Landing, and that's when I knew we would never be."

The words were like a bell signaling a death toll. Fortune was against it all.

And just like that, it all fell into place. That tear on Roland's cheek so many years ago had been because of me.

I'd broken his heart without even knowing it. I'd shattered it into a million pieces—had destroyed him and not even known it. Heat rose in my cheeks for the shame of what I'd done.

I was like Mason, completely unaware and lost to myself. The reflection in the mirror was ghastly, but the reality was so clear. Roland was too good for me.

Pulling his hand to my chest I watched as he turned to me. I'd thought I had opened myself to him throughout all of this trip—that I had been the only one to offer pieces of myself, but I'd been wrong. He'd been sharing himself with me all along and I had been too blind, too stupid to see it.

"Why—why didn't you tell me?" I said around jagged breaths.

He gave a short laugh and rested his hand along my cheek again. "Because, I was afraid if I ever shared these pieces of myself with you, I would never be whole again when you left. And if you stayed, I knew I would be the reason you didn't get to experience the world like you've always wanted." This time one of those tears escaped and it tore at my heart. I was the cause of this.

Roland continued with his confession—his words etching their way into my heart and I wasn't sure if I would ever be able to put it back together. We were long past standing on the solid ground of friendship. Perhaps these feelings had been coursing between us for years, but in my fear, I had pushed it all away. I wanted to flee, even now, as his thumb brushed away my tears.

"That night I knew I could never have you, so I forced myself to simply be your friend. I lied to myself and said it was better than nothing, but the pain of knowing you would never see me as I see you was enough to strangle all hope from me. But I forced myself to keep going, to take pleasure in being your friend, all the while knowing that you would end up with Mason, or someone like him, never knowing how I felt." He struggled for breath. "And that was the worst part. You've been so blind, Dani. So unaware of how I've felt for you, how I want you." His hands twisted in my hair. My tears were flowing freely now and I didn't know if words would be able to express what was happening in my chest, because I knew the end of this was coming soon.

I'd been right before. The door was open and there was no going back. But now I saw there was no door—here on this beach it had been destroyed in our confessions. My fear and his longing had broken what remained of our friendship, morphing it into this new creature that could never flourish.

Tears ran off my chin, flowing too quickly and I had to wipe at my nose. "I'm sorry, Roland." I swallowed. He didn't know how sorry.

He was already shaking his head. "Don't be sorry, that's not why I told you this. I—I just needed you to know why I was wrong to lead us to this place."

I thought he meant the beach and I glanced around us as though expecting something to appear. Roland shook his head again; all traces of his dear smiles had disappeared along with his tears. Instead, the determination in his eyes was back.

A different kind of determination.

"I tried to make you see that your heart belongs here," he placed one of my hands over his heart, "but I was wrong."

No, it was I who was wrong. So blind. Even in the airport with our stupid bet, he'd been trying to tell me he loved me.

"I've always been a dreamer, Dani, but not like you. I enjoy my simple life in Landing, near home where I can take care of my mom. I've seen firsthand what can happen if a relationship thwarts a dream."

Thinking of Roland's dad, I finally understood what he meant. He saw me as someone like his father, someone with a restless spirit, wanting to fly, but too afraid to try. I was a caged bird. My lips trembled as my shameful cowardice was laid bare.

"Forgive me for even putting this between us," he whispered, drawing me close. Wrapped in his arms I clung to him, trying to hold the pieces of myself together. For him, I could be strong. "You were the dream I never thought I could have," he admitted softly.

For how long we stood there, I didn't know, but as our trembling breaths stilled the distance between our hearts widened. Even if I could put my fears aside, he wouldn't let me be with him. He'd heard me confess the longings of my heart that night so many years ago, and to him, adventure was a bridge he couldn't cross.

It was enough, for now, to simply hold one another.

The air seemed to dip even colder and when my shivering became more than noticeable, Roland turned us back toward the house. The path seemed darker now and as we slipped inside, he squeezed my hand without looking at me and left for his room. All alone in the dark, I waited for the door to his bedroom to close, and then I broke.

Silently I shattered, letting my heart shatter into pieces I couldn't gather.

When I could finally stand again, I reached the guest bedroom and packed my bags. I'd fled from Landing in the middle of the night, why couldn't I do it again?

A quick search online found a rental car and a ticket for a plane ride home. Roland would have to spend the rest of his time with his grandparents alone.

Hastily leaving them a note on the kitchen table, I slipped out the door in the early mid-morning light and walked the trail to town. A cab took me to the rental place a few towns over and by the time I was driving toward Inverness, my phone had been clicked off as well as all thought.

I was headed home—to a place where pain could drift away.

As I boarded my connecting flight in Edinburgh, I thrust all that had happened behind me. I would not spend the next hours thinking of Roland, of hating my cowardly heart, of wishing I was in love with him and that we could simply be friends. No, I would force myself to stay focused on what was ahead and not on what was behind.

But all the while, I knew I was letting practicality justify my fears. And it was enough, but for the thought that Charlotte Lucas would have done the same.

CHAPTER 24

"This is just perfect. You've captured the essence of it." Mrs. Kent's voice exclaimed from the speaker on my phone.

"Good, I'm so glad you like it."

"We love it! Mr. Kent said it was worth every penny. It's just what we wanted."

"I'm so pleased to hear that," I said, smiling. It felt odd to smile. At least my eyes were currently dry.

"Send over the final invoice and Mr. Kent will have that taken care of. And make sure you send us all of your receipts."

"Yes ma'am, I did."

"Okay, we wanted to make sure." I could hear the smile in Mrs. Kent's voice and remembered the crinkles around her eyes as she grinned. "And if ever you are in town, you will have a free place to stay. Mr. Kent wants to meet you." There was such love in her voice for her husband.

"I'd like to meet him too," I said, leaning back in my desk chair, the springs squeaked. Perhaps a trip to the Kent's Bed & Breakfast would be in order. It was more than your average place to stay. Each piece of décor had been perfectly selected to evoke the essence of a British country house. It was sure to be a sought-after retreat.

We said our goodbyes over the phone and silence filled my loft apartment—the all too familiar quiet of these past days. Curled in my chair, I stared at my computer as I had for so many hours since returning to

Landing. But at least then I'd had work to do. The final touches for the Kent's was my final project. Pulling up my task list I realized just how far ahead I was.

It should have given me some peace of mind, but it didn't.

Unwillingly, my eyes drifted toward the window and the setting sun. Across town, I spotted Roland's shop. Even thinking of him sent a sharp pang through my chest.

It had been eight days. Eight days of silence between us.

Since first meeting Roland in high school, we'd never gone so long without at least making contact once. The silence between us was evident. There was a gaping hole and for the first few days, I hadn't wanted to acknowledge it.

Now I had no choice.

Pulling my reheated beef stew from the microwave, I sat down at an empty table. The steam rose toward me, and I wanted to enjoy it—enjoy something, but I couldn't. It felt as though something inside of me was broken.

Grabbing my phone, I sent a quick text to Anna. I knew she would be home and I couldn't stand the thought of another night alone. Sure enough, her response to come over was the relief I needed. Another voice, another's thoughts—something to keep me entertained.

Throwing some clothes into a backpack, I gathered my things, allowing myself one short glance out my window. His light was on.

A pang shot through my heart. I didn't know what hurt more, the silence or the fact that he was home and I still hadn't heard from him. Sniffing back tears, I called Chandler and we left town for the thirty-minute drive to Anna's.

"Hey!" Anna waved from the porch, Jackson on her hip. My youngest nephew was still nursing, at only four months old he still seemed to have grown twice in size since I'd last seen him a mere two weeks ago.

"Hey," I said, keeping my eyes focused on Jackson. Babies were an easy distraction, in their eyes was only love. No pity, no worry, just acceptance of life as it was in the moment.

Chandler immediately made himself at home, curling up on the rug in the middle of the floor. All in the house was quiet aside from Jackson's coos and awes as he watched Chandler. So far Anna and her husband had decided against getting a dog. Although, the last time I was over for dinner Kevin sounded like he was ready for a puppy.

All the other kids were already asleep and as I sat on the floor beside Chandler, ankles crossed and warm winter socks covering my freezing toes, I ran my fingers through his fur while avoiding the obvious.

"So?" Anna said, joining me on the floor, her eyes on Jackson as he swung his arms at awkward angles.

"So," I nodded, and then I looked up.

There were years in her eyes. Memories of shattered moments—mine and hers, flickering there. We'd met in this place often over the years. I remembered sitting on this very floor when she'd found out her second child had passed in her womb. I hadn't known what to say then and had remained silent beside her.

Sometimes, in the broken stillness of a weeping soul, words couldn't suffice. But having someone to lean against in the hurt was everything.

Smiling through my tears, I shrugged my shoulders, helpless. "Sorry," I mumbled, wiping at my eyes as the tears flowed freely.

Chandler moved his head against my leg and I scratched under his chin just the way he liked. Anna didn't say anything, letting me gather myself for as long as I needed.

"Is Kevin here?" I asked.

Anna nodded. "Already in bed. He's watching some murder documentary."

"Sounds like him," I smiled, weakly.

The silence stretched, my breaths becoming steadier. I could do this; I would do this. There was an aching need to get the trapped words in my chest out in the open.

"I really messed up," my voice broke. Those words snapped the dam that I had been struggling to hold up. In my mind I was back on that beach—the place where I had experienced more freedom than ever before, daring to ride across the sand and let adventure seep into my soul. It was the special place where I'd begun to see Roland as he truly was.

Even thinking of his name yanked on the strings of my heart. Sometimes I hated that I was a person who felt so deeply. There were times where I thought it would be easier to simply go through life in a balanced state—but that wasn't me. I was passionate, and that was something that was at once a curse and a blessing.

"How so?" Anna asked softly. Jackson was struggling to try and roll from his back to his stomach.

"I've never felt like this before." I pressed a hand to my chest. "I just keep thinking that the reason I am where I am is because of me." Sucking in a breath, I pushed my hair back. "You know, Roland saw it too. He thinks I'm too afraid sometimes, that I need to take a risk."

Anna nodded but didn't say anything.

"And I know that, and I've tried, but I'm always afraid to take the leap. It's just I'm afraid of what's on the other side."

Anna looked a little confused. "What do you mean?"

"He told me he loved me." There I said it.

Anna blinked. "So, you finally realized it."

I half-laughed at her bluntness. "It was that obvious?"

Anna smiled, tickling Jackson's tummy. "You can see it in the way he looks at you. I did try and tell you a few times, but you never seemed interested."

It was my turn to nod. Anna was right. She had suggested I try dating Roland a few times, but I hadn't wanted to risk our friendship, and my focus had been on Mason.

"I've been so blind," I admitted.

"Maybe, but now that you know, what are you going to do about it?"

I shrugged, wiping at my nose. "I don't know. I've tried thinking about what it might be like, but I don't know if I can be that way with him. There's attraction there, but I don't want to lose his friendship, you know?"

"And what if you don't lose it? What if it only redefines your relationship?"

"Maybe," even to my ears I sounded doubtful. "This was just the line I had been trying to avoid crossing for years. We've always been close," I explained, "but now everything is different. I don't know how to just be his friend anymore. Too much has happened."

Anna met my eyes with a knowing look—one that made me want to cringe away and spill my guts at the same time.

I broke our gaze and sucked in a deep, controlling breath. "I just thought everything would be so different by now, and I feel like a failure." My heart was spilling more than I realized. "It wasn't supposed to be like this. We were supposed to have kids at the same time, and I feel like I failed you— that I let you down."

When Anna didn't say anything, I finally met her eyes once more. She was staring at me, shocked. "You don't really think that do you?"

"Partially."

Anna shook her head. "Danielle, you place way too much pressure on yourself."

"Well, who else is going to? My life is so selfish, Anna. Like everything in my life revolves around my schedule, my work, my time with friends, and nothing ever changes. I'm stuck and I don't know what to do to get out."

"Yes, you do."

My head snapped up. It was rare that Anna challenged me. Of the two of us, she was shyer, and yet, she was one of the strongest people I knew.

"I think you've known what you need to do for a long time, and all this," she waved a hand at my teary eyes, "should be telling you more about your heart than I ever could."

Blinking rapidly, my lip trembling, I nodded. "I don't know if I can risk our friendship, but I don't want to lose him, Anna. I love him as a friend, but not in the way he wants. I don't think I can be what he deserves." The admission took my breath away.

We sat in silence again for a long time. Jackson's eyes had closed and he was lulling off to sleep. Anna quietly rose and crossed the room to sit next to me, our backs leaning against the couch. "Why don't you tell me what happened."

"If I can get through it," I laughed half-heartedly.

"You have to have some pictures," she offered.

I dug into my purse for my phone, thankful for the distraction she provided. "Where should I start?"

"How about at the beginning, like why you left in the middle of the night anyway?"

I laughed again and then nodded. I could do this.

As I spoke my tears dried. Anna made some tea and I continued to tell her all about Highclere Castle and then the surprise of seeing Roland. She smiled at all the right moments, never interrupting and simply listening. Eventually, I handed her my phone so she could swipe through the pictures as I tried to describe the beauty of Chatsworth House. I was attempting to accurately portray Alexander when her smile broadened—her thumb swiping back and forth, right and then left. I couldn't see what was on my phone, but I suddenly knew she was no longer listening to me.

"What?" I asked leaning forward.

"I knew it," Anna said, holding out my phone to me.

There it was, the picture Alexander had taken of me and Roland as we stood on the porch overlooking the large reflecting pool at Chatsworth House. Roland had his arm around me, and I remembered when he had poked me in the side. I was laughing, and the look in his eyes was much the same as the one he'd given me on the beach. He loved me, every part of my being knew it.

That line had been crossed, not only with our actions but with the confession of his heart.

Anna was watching me. I glanced up at her. "He loves you, but look."

She swiped to the right and I stared. This picture had been taken a mere second after the first. Roland was laughing now, his eyes closed and his head thrown back slightly, but my focus was pulled elsewhere, to this depiction of one candid moment in my life. There I was, looking up at Roland, beaming—my eyes brimming with an emotion that was all too easy to name.

I gasped slightly as the pieces fell into place. Was I so blind to even my own heart?

"You love him," Anna whispered.

I couldn't speak. Roland had been right all along. My heart did belong with him. Placing a hand over my mouth, I turned to Anna, my fingers shaking. "I didn't realize."

"That's why it hurts so much."

We sat quietly. "It's brutal."

Anna choked out a laugh at that. "Love is." And yet she was smiling. "But, I will tell you it's worth all the pain and fear in the world."

"So, you think I should tell him?"

Anna smiled in answer.

"But I haven't spoken to him since I left Scotland."

"And?"

"And...what if he won't listen to me?"

She pursed her lips. "Will you honestly be able to live with yourself if you never try? Do you want to live with the regret of never telling him and having to watch as he moves on?"

I knew she wasn't trying to cause me pain, but it did all the same. The foggy mist of a possible future pulled at my heartstrings—a smokescreen of Roland marrying someone else, having children, and continuing to live nearby. Would I be able to withstand seeing him that way? Of no longer having him as part of my life? As a part of my family?

It was why this hurt so much. He was embedded into the deepest parts of me. He'd seen and accepted my most vulnerable self, and in turn, I'd done the same.

The confusion of that night on the trampoline flitted through my mind. I hadn't known it then, but that night had changed us. We'd become something in that moment—we'd seen the depths of one another and developed an understanding. Unknowingly, I'd been falling for him ever since.

It was as clear as glass to me now. With him, I was the best version of myself. I wasn't Danielle, confused and worried. I was Dani—simply Dani, and I hoped he would have me. Fear lingered, but perhaps I could take the leap. He'd challenged me to jump once, perhaps, just this once I would be able to fly.

"You know how you always say you're like Charlotte Lucas?" Anna prompted.

I nodded.

"Well, doesn't she say something about love needing proper encouragement?"

I bit my lip. Charlotte did say something of that sort. Perhaps, I had been so wrong all along. The urge to remedy all of it was enough to make me want to hop in my car and race back to Landing in the middle of the night. What if I was too late? I worried my lip.

"Wait for tomorrow," Anna patted my hand, reading my thoughts in a way only a sister could, "then go tell him."

I squeezed her fingers. "Thank you."

She winked and settled next to my shoulder, a yawn parting her lips. "Anytime."

CHAPTER 25

I was armed for battle. More a battle of the heart and internal fear than a battle against the world.

After a nearly restless night and a day spent playing with my nieces and nephews, I found myself back at my loft and staring out the window at Roland's shop. The day had seemed to move faster than I would have thought possible.

Chandler nudged my hand and I scratched behind his ear just the way he liked. I could do this.

The ledge was getting closer, and I knew I had to take the leap. Wasn't that what this had all been about from the beginning?

Down below two figures walked by. I spotted Mason's blonde hair and saw a woman's arm hooked through his. They were laughing and huddled together in private conversation as they walked away.

I smiled gently, almost mournful for the lies I had spent years forcing myself to believe. Mason had been a whimsical idea. A vague dream founded in imperfect imagination of what I thought I could conjure.

From my vantage point at my desk, a light suddenly glowed across the town square. *Roland.*

He was my reality. He was home.

Was it possible for a stomach to do summersaults?

Steadying my breath, I reached for the sweatshirt that had stowed its way into my bags. I'd left Scotland in such a hurry that I'd accidentally thrown the sweatshirt in with my other things. It was only fitting I would have something of his to wear.

Maybe it was my imagination, but it still smelled of him. The warm pine scent conjuring memories—his hands caressing my face, his arms drawing me close, his lips on mine—all of it tingled my skin. But his words on the beach threatened all calm.

He'd dared me to jump, and now I knew I at least had wings. I loved him, but would it be enough?

Taking a deep breath, I kissed Chandler's head for good luck and made my way out the door with the package in hand. The wind was sharp and cool, whispering memories of that Scottish beach—faded whims reminding me not to falter this time.

All was familiar as I approached Roland's shop; the polished furniture on display, the logo glinting on the glass window, and the wood-crafted sign depicting the shop's hours. Inhaling, I reached for the door handle and pulled. The bell trilled.

"Hey," Cole said from behind the counter. He had a pencil stuck behind his ear and he was typing into one of the computers. He cocked his head sideways in a beckoning motion. "He's in the back."

I nodded my thanks, too afraid to talk.

As always, the music was blaring, the beat bouncing off the walls in a manner that disguised the sharp whir of the table saw. The sight of Roland made my heart jump, flutter, and then restart.

My hands were shaking, I knew they would, and yet my lips lifted into a soft smile, watching as he moved along his workbench. Once he had told me that when designing I got this deep crease between my brows, he'd been amused by it. Oh, how had I not realized his feelings for me then?

Shaking my head, I watched him work. His hands glided along the wood, testing and rechecking, each move precise and careful, but it was the downturn of his mouth that pulled at those tender heartstrings—the ones that had been ripped and shredded on that beach.

Never before had I seen him look like this while working. His craftsmanship came from his inmost soul, it was the place where he was most himself, relaxed and calm. But anyone looking at Roland right now could tell he wasn't at ease.

I wondered and almost knew that there would be a fire in his eyes if he looked at me. Whether it was a fire of anger or passion, I didn't know.

Standing in my leggings, athletic shoes and his sweatshirt, I suddenly felt underprepared for what I was about to do. But I couldn't choose to back down any longer. To not make a move was a choice—and it wasn't one I wanted to make anymore.

As though my thoughts were reverberating in the room, Roland finished a cut and glanced up. The saw stopped and without looking directly at me, he leaned over to turn the music down. With one swift motion, he removed his protective glasses and gloves.

Was it possible for a room to grow still? Could he hear the erratic beat of my heart? It didn't seem possible that he couldn't.

All words were lost as I stood there uncomfortably, uncertainty reigning. There had been a time when nothing was lost between us, but the span of eight days, eight simple days, seemed like an eternity.

A precipice lingered. I could choose to jump or flee.

Swallowing, my one step forward felt like a plunge from the ledge.

I placed the package on his workbench and slid it toward him, grateful to have a physical barrier between us. He stared at it for a moment and I wondered if he would even reach for it, and then, he looked up.

Fire. I had been right before, it was fire. But not just anger or passion, there was hurt, deep and terrifying hurt. Tears pricked my eyes. I was the reason for that pain.

Knowing his heart was as raw as mine gave me some strength. Sometimes, dwelling in pain with another was enough to bring comfort.

Reaching forward, I edged the package closer, pleading with my eyes. He grasped for it and stood awkwardly. Wondering what to do with my hands when there were no pockets to be found, I clasped them together to still their shaking.

He removed the wrapping from the frame and turned it over. I knew what rested behind that glass. It was the picture of him laughing at Chatsworth, the one that had made me realize my feelings for him.

Holding my breath, I waited and waited. He stared, at the photo and I waited for something in his expression to change even as his fingers slid along the wooden frame. When he looked up, the look in his eyes punching straight to my gut.

It was time.

"You love me," I said softly, my voice cracking. There was a wetness in his eyes, rimmed with raw wounds, but there was also a lifeline—a glimmer of hope. "But now you know." I gestured toward the picture and when I spoke again, my voice broke with emotion. "I love you too, Roland. And I know you think that to be with you is giving up on a life of adventure, but," I swallowed heavily, trying to push through and tell him all the words that had been stored up in my heart, so long undetected. "But, loving you is the greatest adventure I can think of."

There it was, the leap.

My heart was out on the table between us, ready to be ripped to shreds if he decided the risk was too great. I watched as he blinked, his thumb rubbing the side of that frame over and over again.

Tears threatened. "Say something," I breathed, wiping at my eyes.

He didn't speak—and quite suddenly I realized he didn't need to. For there in his gaze was the fire from before, but it had changed. Hope had kindled, sparking into a burning flame of passion.

Roland placed the frame down on the workbench and eased around the table. Each step seemed to take him an eternity, and I hated that tears built in my eyes and rolled down my cheeks. Everything in me told me to flee, to turn and run, but I couldn't. I wouldn't.

For the first time, I had leaped and now I would stand my ground.

Blinking away the tears, I wiped at my eyes and laughed at my awkwardness. "Sorry," I mumbled, around constricting breaths as he drew closer. And closer still.

He reached for me, caressing my face as though I was the most breakable doll in the world. His eyes roved over me, searching into my own for the confirmation of my words. All the love I had for him seemed to spill over in his searching—unbridled affection poured forth.

It was as though as soon as I realized my love for him, it broke free from the restraint I had placed on my heart. No longer could it hold back the tidal wave. It was a rushing current too long ignored.

A slow smile curled the edges of his lips, and that was all. I was seen, truly seen, and accepted as I was. And that was a beautiful thing—to be known and still be loved.

One single tear fell from his right eye and I reached for it, wiping it away with my fingers. "Roland," I whispered.

It was like his name on my lips snapped the leash that held him bound. Before I had the chance to react, his mouth was on mine, capturing me in a kiss that sent fire all the way to my toes. He pushed forward, his steps bringing my back up against the wall. It was a retreat, but as long as he was with me, I would consider it a conjoined effort.

Fingers running through my hair, I fell into his arms and let all fears fall away as he showered me with an affection I hadn't known existed. Even in Scotland, he'd kept himself on a tether, but this was different. Here, now, with him, he let all restraint go and kissed me with a resounding confirmation of the love I now knew beat in his heart.

"Dani," he whispered, the sound of his voice doing something to my heart. I was all melted inside. "Dani."

For how long we declared our love for one another I didn't know, time no longer had meaning, all the world was him. Eventually, his lips slowed and I ducked down to rest my head against his chest. There beneath the worn gray of his shirt was the erratic beat of his heart.

He ran a hand up and down my back sending shivers along my spine. "Are you sure?" The question seemed to pain him. But if I knew Roland, my dear, selfless Roland, he would have to be absolutely certain before taking away anyone's hopes or dreams.

I nodded against his chest and his arms tightened around me. I could remain in his embrace for days, the warmth and comfort there was a pleasure unknown.

Drawing back slightly, I wanted him to know beyond the shadow of a doubt what it was I felt. My words on the beach were too clear, the shards of fragmented glass that could pierce the heart. Never could I take them back, but I could reframe them.

His arms loosened slightly as I drew back to look at him. Making sure he met my gaze for this, I placed my hand along his cheek, the subtle stubble there slightly pricking.

"I realized I loved you all along." My voice cracked again and I cleared it, smiling when Roland laughed, his chest rising and falling beneath my fingers. "You're my best friend, and I'm more myself with you than anyone else. I do love you."

The deep brown of his eyes warmed. "You are my home."

Those four words settled deep within my heart, breaking all walls and all fears. Pure abounding joy poured from me, and I tucked my head against his chest once more, perfectly content to simply be here in his arms.

"You know what?" I murmured many minutes later.

"Hmm?" he asked, his voice rumbling in his chest.

"You were right."

"About what this time?" Amusement laced his tone.

"My heart does belong here."

His arms loosened and when I pulled back, he rested his forehead against mine. Closing my eyes, I leaned into him as he whispered the sweetest of words.

"Yes, it does."

CHAPTER 26

Three hundred and sixty-five days.

That's how many days had passed since I fled Scotland in the early light of morning. An entire year and so much had changed.

Looking around my loft, I fiddled with the rings on my left hand. One my engagement ring, the other, a simple band. Both were placed by Roland and perfectly circling my finger.

Biting my lip, I stared down and reminisced as I looked at my now empty loft apartment. Outside, my mom and dad were walking Chandler to our new house nearly five minutes away, a short walk from Roland's shop.

Oh, how the wedding preparations and wedding day had flown by. It all seemed a bit like a dream, one I couldn't believe I was still soaring through. But Roland was my tether—the one who held it all together.

Smiling, I stared at the empty kitchen cabinets and rooms. Before the wedding, I had boxed up nearly everything, but then we'd spent our first few months as a married couple in these rooms. Now that Roland had finished renovating our house, we were leaving this space behind.

I found myself quite remiss to let it go and clicked a few pictures on my phone, uncertain of whether or not they would ever be printed. Sometimes it was simply pleasant to document a memory.

There on the wall were five pictures. The first was a photo from high school, beside it was one from our honeymoon at the Kent's Bed & Breakfast, *Charlotte's Parlor*. It really had been every bit as magical as I had anticipated. And then there was our wedding photo between the ones of us at Chatsworth. Roland looking at me, and me at him. Reaching for them, I pulled them off the walls. I don't know why I had waited so long to take them down, perhaps because then it was official. Photographs had a way of making a home a home.

Sighing, I stacked them on top of one another as I heard Roland bounding up the stairs.

"Dani?"

I would never tire of hearing him call for me. "Yes?" I asked, turning, the frames wrapped in my arms.

He was all things light and warm, his hair as dark as ever and his smiles bright and beaming. With his sleeves rolled up to his elbows, my eyes drifted to the strong muscles I knew rested there. A desire stirred within me, one that had been the most pleasant of aching needs since the night of our wedding. Oh, how I thrilled when he took me in his arms.

My cheeks flushing, I forced myself to remain in the moment and not try and hasten the day until evening when our families were gone.

Roland laughed at my blush, knowing me all too well. He placed a rather heavy kiss on my lips, his intent quite obvious. Flustered, I ran a hand through my hair and flipped it over my shoulder. After a few months of marriage, I was still blushing like a young girl.

"Are you ready?" he asked, his voice husky. "To leave, that is."

I smacked his shoulder. "Let me check everything one more time and then I'll lock up."

Roland nodded and I handed him the frames before turning and looking through the kitchen cabinets. Nothing but bare space met my eyes. All was clean and right in the world.

One more quick check of all the corners and I was headed for the stairs when I stopped in my tracks. An envelope lay in the middle of the floor.

The paper crinkled beneath my fingers as I hastened to open the clean pages where a careful, steady hand had scrawled these words.

For my wife,

I have never told you about the morning you left Scotland. Perhaps it is because the pain I felt in that moment was too much to put into words. Even now, I flinch at the memory. I never told you about how I hardly slept, how I heard the stairs creak as you reached your room. I didn't tell you how I battled with myself nearly all through the night on whether or not I should go to you. And I did. In the early morning, I knocked on your door. Perhaps we missed each other only by a few minutes. To hear your recounting of the story, it couldn't have been far apart.

I can't tell you how much it hurt when I realized you were gone. Words wouldn't suffice.

Do you remember telling me how you were afraid all the time? My darling, Dani, ever since I met you, I was afraid of losing you. And the pain that came was enough that I knew I had been right in my fear, but that is all part of our story, isn't it?

You see, when you entered my shop and told me you loved me, my world suddenly became whole again. Before me, I saw a woman who finally realized her strength, who finally saw herself the way I always had, and I knew that together we could face the world. You once told to me you felt like Charlotte Lucas, forever alone and overlooked—afraid that all adventure in life would pass you by. Well, my dearest, Charlotte, you are wrong.

You were never overlooked or passed by, and as for adventure, this past year has only been the beginning of the journey.

Now come downstairs, my dearest Danielle Charlotte Harmon, my wife, and together we will start the next chapter of our lives. To have and to hold, now and always.

I love you, Dani, with all my heart.

Your husband,

Roland

It took me more than a few tries to read through the entire letter due to the tears coursing down my cheeks. They were tears of joy for what was to come and for what had been left behind.

Wiping away at my eyes, I smiled and hurried down the stairs with his letter in hand. He was leaning against the truck, his hands tucked into the front of his jeans. When I met his gaze, I held the letter up.

"Thank you," I mouthed, uncertain if my voice would work.

Roland saw all the pieces of me—all the fear that had fallen away, and still, I was his and he was mine.

Of all the stories and books I'd read, the endings always moved toward a happily ever after. But this was real life—reality, not a dream. Difficult times were sure to come our way, but that was part of the adventure.

In the stories, Mr. Darcy and Elizabeth were married, Cinderella got the prince, Belle and the Beast broke the spell, and Anne and Gilbert finally came to love one another. And that was the end, a story with a conclusion.

And perhaps that was all we were, a conclusion of love finally finding one another. Love that was willing to endure and move forward.

I knew then that stories couldn't cover all of it, the chapters had to end. But the exciting part about reality was each chapter led to the next.

As we piled into the truck and rolled away from my loft, I knew the short drive was only the beginning of a new and exciting chapter. Glancing out the window I whispered my goodbyes to the Dani who had been so afraid. And then I offered up one more.

Goodbye, Charlotte. I thought, and smiled to myself as I knew my fear of never taking the chance to risk love was in my past.

Grasping Roland's hand as he drove, he squeezed my fingers—his smile warming me to my toes.

Onward. The adventure of life together awaited.

THE END

Meaghan Rauscher's debut as an author was the *Droplets* trilogy. With the first book written while in high school, she proceeded to complete her mermaid trilogy throughout college. Now a seasoned author, Meaghan lives in her hometown of Augusta, GA where she works in ministry while finding moments to escape and write. *My Dearest Charlotte* was the result of extra time in 2020 and a personal challenge to write a standalone modern romance.

For those avid readers who are wondering about the second installment of *Roar of the Realm* series, Meaghan is currently work on book two and she is just as interested to find out where the story is going!

Instagram: @MeaghanRauscher
Facebook: Meaghan Rauscher, Author

www.ingramcontent.com/pod-product-compliance
Lightning Source LLC
Chambersburg PA
CBHW021036130626
46552CB00005B/1877